A MAN SHOT DOWNWARD FROM THE BRIDGE AND THE
MACHINE BEGAN CLICKING. —*Page* 146

The Moving Picture Boys.

THE MOVING PICTURE BOYS

OR

The Perils of a Great City Depicted

BY

VICTOR APPLETON

AUTHOR OF "THE MOVING PICTURE BOYS IN THE WEST," "TOM SWIFT
AND HIS MOTOR CYCLE," "TOM SWIFT AND HIS AIRSHIP," "TOM
SWIFT AND HIS GREAT SEARCHLIGHT," ETC.

ILLUSTRATED

NEW YORK
GROSSET & DUNLAP
PUBLISHERS

CONTENTS

iv CONTENTS

THE MOVING PICTURE BOYS

CHAPTER I

TO THE RESCUE

"HELLO, Blake! Have you heard the news?"

"News? What news, Joe?" and the second speaker, a boy like the first, leaned over the fence surrounding a field of corn, in which he had been hoeing.

"Didn't you hear it? Why, a moving picture man is coming to town!"

"A moving picture man?"

"Yes; but that isn't all the news. I've lost my job."

"Lost your job! Say, look here, Joe Duncan, are you fooling me?"

"Not a bit of it. It's all true."

"But what has a moving picture man coming to town got to do with you losing your job?"

"Nothing, only those are the two latest pieces of news, and I thought you'd like to hear 'em."

"I do—I mean I'm sorry about you losing your place, of course. I was wondering what brought you around this time of the morning."

"That's right—I'm through working. But I see you're not."

"No, hoeing this corn is a bigger task than I thought it was. But I guess I'll finish some time this morning, and then I hope Uncle Jonathan will let me have a little rest. In fact, I'm sure he will."

"What makes you think so? He isn't in the habit of letting his farm work go, is he?"

"No, Joe; but something has happened in the last few days that will make a big change for him—and me, too, for that matter. I can't talk about it yet, or I'd tell you. But I'm afraid I'm going to have a harder row to hoe than any in this cornfield. But what happened between you and Mr. Bradley? Did you have a quarrel?"

"No, but he's lost some money he calculated·on getting, and he says he can't afford to keep me any longer. I'm through after to-day, but he was decent enough to tell me I could have the rest of the time off to look for another place. I don't know where to look, that's a fact; and I was sort of hoping perhaps your uncle might want to hire me."

"I'm afraid not, Joe," and Blake Stewart looked at his friend, Joe Duncan, with sympathetic eyes. "In fact I know he doesn't want any more help, Joe. I can tell you why, in a day or so, but not now. So you'll have to look somewhere else for work."

"Yes, I guess so, and the worst of it is that all the farmers around here have their help engaged for the season. I may have to travel quite a way to get a job, and I haven't got much money to travel on."

"I'm sorry for you, Joe," spoke Blake, "and I wish I could help you; but I'm likely to be in the same boat myself soon. Have you any plans in view?"

"Yes, Blake, I have!"

There was a new and sudden determination in the lad's tone, and his chum looked at him in some surprise.

"What is it?" he asked. "Have you thought of some other place you can go to?"

"Yes, I have. And it's down to the creek, fishing! I might as well be killed for a sheep as a lamb, as the old saying has it. I'm out of work, and don't know when I'll get more, but I'm going to have a good time for once in my life! I'm going fishing. I've been slaving all winter and spring. Now I'm going to take it a little easier, even if it's for only a half day.

"But say, Blake, you don't look any too happy yourself," he added, quickly, as if to change the subject. "Why don't you come along? The day's just right for catching the big ones. I think they'll bite well. We can dig some worms and catch a mess of fish for supper. Come on!"

"I wish I could, Joe. As you say, I'm not feeling any too joyous myself, but I promised Uncle Jonathan I'd hoe this corn, and I don't like to disappoint him, though he'll never get any benefit from it. Still, I might take——"

"I'll tell you what I'll do, Blake!" exclaimed Joe. "I'll give you a hand with that corn myself. We can finish up the rest of the rows in an hour, and that will give us plenty of time to fish. How's that?"

"I don't like to impose on you."

"It isn't imposing. It's no fun going fishing alone, when, by helping you, I can get a chum. Got an extra hoe?"

"Yes. There's one over in the fence corner. Uncle Jonathan was using it until he got tired."

Joe Duncan leaped the topmost rail, found the implement, and was soon hoeing away at the corn, which was about a foot high. The dirt was pulled in a heap about the foot of the stalks to better support them, and also to loosen up the soil, and make it moist.

"Two rows more, and we'll be through!" exclaimed Joe, after the lads had passed the length of the field several times. "Your uncle will let you go, won't he, after you get through?"

"Yes; this is the last chore I have until night."

"I guess we can get the worms here. And we can stop at Mr. Bradley's place on our way to the creek, while I get my pole. I'm going to have one good day's fishing, and then I'll look for another place."

"And I——" began Blake, and then he stopped suddenly.

"What's the matter?" asked Joe, in some surprise.

"Oh, nothing. Or, rather, I'll tell you later. But say, Joe, when you get your row finished you go on to your house and get your pole. I'll dig the worms and call for you."

"All right. That's a go!" and Joe made the dirt fairly fly with the hoe, so anxious was he to finish. A little later he stood the implement up where he had found it, and called:

"Done! I'm off. Come as soon as you can, Blake."

"I will," and then, with a wave of his hand to

his chum, Blake kept on with the few hills remaining in the last row on which he was working. Soon he had finished, and, taking the two hoes to the farmhouse of his uncle, he proceeded to dig some worms.

A little later the two lads, with fishpoles over their shoulders, were trudging down the country lane toward the creek where they swam, fished and skated in season.

"Oh, say, Joe!" exclaimed Blake, when they had walked on some distance, talking of various subjects. "What was that you said about a moving picture man coming to town?"

"That's right; one is coming, and soon, too."

"A moving picture man, eh? Do you mean he's going to give a show here?"

"No; I wish he was. I'd like to go to one first rate. I saw an exhibition once, down at Paddington, and it sure was slick! It was really wonderful, the way things happened. Why, one man was run over by an auto, and his legs were taken off, and a minute later a doctor stuck them on, and the man got up and danced as well as ever."

"Get out!"

"It's a fact. Of course, there was some trick about it, and I'd like to know how it was done. These moving pictures are such wonderful things. I haven't seen very many, though."

"Me either, and when you first mentioned about a moving picture man coming here, I was hoping we'd get a chance to see some."

"No such luck! Fayetteburg is too small a place to make a moving picture place pay. A man would go bankrupt. But it seems there is good scenery around here, and some concern wants to get views of it."

"Who was telling you that?"

"I heard it down at the hotel. Jenks, the liveryman, said a rig had been engaged from him to take the moving picture man and his camera out in the country somewhere."

"That sounds interesting. I'd like to see some moving pictures being taken, as long as we can't see any thrown on the screen. But, Joe, it doesn't seem as if any concern would come away out here just to get views of scenery. They could do that nearer New York, and I understand that a number of the firms that make the films have places there."

"Oh, it isn't just scenery they're going to take. They just want that for a sort of groundwork— background, I guess they call it. There are some actors and actresses coming out with the moving picture man, and they're going to pose, or do something, while he works the camera. I don't know just what it is, for Jenks didn't know himself, but there was a lot of talk about it down at the hotel."

"I should think there would be. It sounds more interesting than ever. I'd like to see those actors. Whereabouts do you think the pictures will be taken?"

"I don't know. Didn't think to ask, I was so bothered about going to lose my place. Well, maybe I'll get another before summer is over and I have used up my bank account," and Joe laughed frankly, though he was obviously worried.

"I hope so," spoke Blake. "But if we're going to do any fishing, we'd better get a hustle on. Let's take the short cut to the creek; through this field."

"This is old man Hounson's property," objected Joe.

"I know it, but if he doesn't see us cut across it he can't say anything. Besides, it's nothing but pasture, and we can't hurt it."

"I know it, but sometimes he lets that old black bull of his in here, and the beast is as ugly as they make 'em. I don't want him after me."

"Nor I," admitted Blake. "But I don't see anything of him," he went on, as he stood on the rail fence and surveyed the field. "Let's take a chance. It'll save us nearly half a mile."

"All right, I'm with you. Only, if the beast chases us, don't say I didn't warn you. He may be lying down over in that clump of trees."

"I guess not. Anyhow, we can soon get across."

They climbed the fence and started over the pasture, now and then looking back for a sign of the savage bull, that more than once had chased trespassers on Mr. Hounson's property; or, rather, to be more correct, had chased them off. But the lads saw nothing of the animal.

They had almost reached the farther fence, and because of their interest in talking of the prospective visit of the moving picture man, they had forgotten to be on the watch.

Suddenly Joe, hearing a thud of feet behind him, gave a hasty glance over his shoulder and yelled:

"Look out, Blake! Here he comes! Run for it!"

"The sly old fox!" cried Blake. "He sneaked up on us without making a sound. Now he thinks he has us."

Both boys broke into a run, and the bull, seeing that he was observed, gave a lusty bellow and galloped toward them.

"Not this time, old chap!" cried Blake, as he

reached the fence and swung himself across. Joe did the same, tossing his fishpole over in advance.

The lads were only just in time, for a second later the infuriated animal rushed up, and though he tried to stop himself as he saw the fence, he was not altogether successful, but crashed into it, giving a bellow of pain. For the fence was a stout one, as must needs be to retain such an animal, and the creature had struck it with considerable force.

"That's the time we fooled you," taunted Joe, as he picked up some clods of dirt and pelted the bull with them. This made the animal more angry than ever, and he bellowed and tore up the ground with his powerful hoofs, trying in vain to loosen the fence with his horns and big neck.

"Not this time, old chap!" remarked Blake, as he picked up his pole. "We spilled half the worms, though," he added, as he looked in the can. "They bounced out when I ran."

"Never mind; we can get more under stones," said Joe. "Now for a good rest and some fun fishing."

The boys kept on their way toward the creek, leaving the ugly bull behind. But they were not destined to get any fish that day.

As they reached the creek they looked to see if their favorite place was occupied by any of the other village lads. It seemed to be untenanted, however, and they were making for it when Blake called out in a low voice:

"Look there, Joe!"

"Where?"

"Right by the slippery elm tree. See that boat on the creek?"

"So it is, and a lady in it. A stranger around here, too. And see how well she's dressed."

"That's right. I wonder whose boat that is? Must belong to Mr. Harrington."

"It does. But I wonder what she's doing in it? She hasn't any fishpole, and that boat leaks like a sieve. I wonder if we'd better tell her? She may——"

But Joe did not have time to finish the sentence, for at that moment the woman stood up in the boat, threw her arms over her head, and with a shriek fell into the sluggish waters of the creek.

"Overboard!" yelled Blake, flinging his fishpole to one side. "She's fallen in, Joe!"

"That's right, and we've got to get her out! Come on! We'll rescue her!"

The two boys, only pausing to pull off their loose shoes, dashed for the stream, in the middle of which could be seen the woman struggling, while the boat floated slowly off.

CHAPTER II

A SMASHUP

"CAN you see her, Joe?" cried Blake, as they paused for an instant on the bank of the stream.

"No—yes I can, too! There she is, floating into the deep eddy! Come on!"

But before the lads could leap in there came a hail to them from a spot a little distance away, and on the same side of the creek as they themselves were.

"Hold on!" cried a man's voice. "Don't go to the rescue. It's all right!"

"All right?" indignantly demanded Blake, as he looked at the man. "How can she be all right when she's drowning?"

"Come on!" yelled Joe. "She's going down for the second time!"

"Don't jump! You'll spoil everything!" cried the man. And as the boys looked at him in wonder they were aware of a curious buzzing, clicking sound; and they saw that the stranger was standing beside a box-like contrivance mounted on three legs, and turning a handle fastened to it. Hardly knowing what it was, yet beginning to guess, the lads paused for an instant.

"Keep back!" warned the man. It's all right!"

"But she—she'll——" began Blake, almost decided, in spite of the warning, to leap in. The woman seemed to be dead already, as she was floating down stream without motion.

"You keep back!" the man ordered, half savagely. "I know what I'm doing. Don't spoil things now."

"Spoil things?" murmured Joe. "I wonder if he's going to see her drown? Can that be some new kind of an automatic life-saving apparatus he's trying?"

Before he could answer his own question, or before Blake could venture an opinion, there was a scurrying in the bushes on the other side of the creek, and a man, apparently a farm hand, for he carried a hoe, leaped out. He paused for an instant on the edge of the stream, and in the glaring sunlight the boys were sure they had never seen him before, though they knew every farmer and hired man for miles around.

"Come on!" yelled the man who had ordered the boys to keep back. "Get her, C. C."

"He's going to save her," murmured Joe.

"I wonder who he is?" mused Blake. "A queer name—'C. C.' Oh, look!"

As the lad spoke, the farm hand made a leap into the water, and with strong and sure strokes swam toward the floating woman.

"That's the way!" yelled the man with the queer machine. "Go to it, C. C. This will make a dandy! A little more action. Splash the water! Make a spray!"

"And—and get my mouth full!" gasped the man in such mournful tones that, even though they feared they were on the verge of a tragedy, Joe and Blake could scarcely help smiling. "I know I'll get cold from this," went on the man. "And be laid up for a week and maybe die. I don't like this for a cent!"

"Oh, cut that stuff out, C. C.," objected the other man. "Can it, Gloomy. Get more action into it! Now you're there! Make a grab for her as if you meant it! That's fine!" he cried, as the swimming man neared the floating woman. "Pull her out now. Easy, Miss Shay. Don't struggle too much. Oh, this will be a dandy!"

"And I know I'll get pneumonia!" murmured the rescuer.

"Can that!" came sternly from the man, and his machine clicked faster than ever. "Get off your lines. Don't you know the audience can often read what you say by the lip motion? Business there, and follow your cues, both of you!"

By this time the man had the woman in his arms, and proceeded to swim to shore with her, while she lay listlessly on his one arm. It was a realistic rescue, and, ere it was concluded, Joe and Blake were made aware of the nature of it.

"Moving pictures!" cried Blake.

"That's it!" agreed his chum.

"We've actually seen some moving pictures being taken," went on Blake, "even though we can't see 'em put on the screen. This is great!"

"I should say yes," agreed Joe. "No wonder that man didn't want us to jump in to the rescue. We'd have spoiled the picture for him."

"But that other fellow jumped in," suggested Blake.

"Oh, that's what he was for. He was just in the right position, with good light and everything."

"I wonder who he is? I don't know any one like him who works on a farm around here."

"He isn't from any farm," declared Joe. "He's an actor, dressed up like a farmer. That's easy to do. He'll take her ashore, bring her around, and maybe in the next picture he'll turn out to be a rich man and marry her. This is a moving picture drama, Blake."

"I guess you're right," spoke his chum. "It's worth seeing, anyhow. I wish we could look at the rest of it. See, he's almost got her ashore."

The rescuer was nearing the opposite bank of the stream, and the man at the moving picture camera, which the boys correctly guessed the apparatus to be, was grinding away at the handle faster than ever, getting thousands of impressions on the roll of sensitive film that traveled back of the lens.

"Good! Good!" the photographer called from time to time. "Very realistic. I'm sure Mr. Ringold will be pleased with this. It's one of the best films I have ever taken for him."

"Yes, it's all right for you!" called the actor who, taking the part of a farmhand, had rescued the lady. "It's all right for you, but what do I get out of it?"

"Why, your salary, of course, C. C.; and that's a bigger one than I get," snapped the photographer on the bank. "Be careful now and don't say anything but your lines when you face the camera. It shows, you know."

"That's all right" continued the man in the water. "I may get my salary; but I'll get the grip sure from being in this water so long. This is a no-good job anyhow. I'm going to resign, if I have any more tank dramas!"

"Oh, forget it, Gloomy!" advised the photographer. "You'll be in dry clothes soon. It's only a little longer, and you'll be ashore. Don't forget to place her down so I can get a good snap of her, and then· do first aid to the injured business. There's only a few yards of film in this reel, and then I'll have to stop and put in another. Go a little livelier, C. C.," and the actor, who appeared to have two nicknames, quickened his strokes.

"Tell the others not to come out until I give the word," warned the photographer. "I don't want this reel spoiled as the other was. Go on, now, that's fine. A good thing the water is deep near shore. You can swim in all the way, and you won't have to crawl, or wade and pretend to swim, the way we did last. When we showed that missing boy picture the audience giggled at the rescue scene, because they could see the water was only about two feet deep. I told Ringold beforehand how it would be, but he wouldn't listen. That's fine!"

"And I'm wetter than a rat!" said the actor, in despairing tones. "No more for mine!"

"Oh, forget it, C. C.," advised the other.

The boys were looking on eagerly, being much interested in the operation of taking moving pictures as well as in the conversation.

"Isn't this great?" cried Blake, enthusiastically.

"It sure is," declared Joe. "I wouldn't have missed it for a whole lot. But there must be some more coming. You heard what he said about telling the others not to come out until he gave the word?"

"Yes. We'll stick around. But as long as we don't have to do any rescue work we might as well put on our shoes."

"That's right. I was wondering what made my feet hurt, but I was so interested I forgot I was in my socks. Look, he's on shore now!"

The rescuer had by this time lifted the form of the actress to the bank. At first the boys were not sure but that she was partly drowned, so still and quiet she lay, but they learned afterward that Miss Shay, which was her stage name, was a clever actress, and was chosen for just such scenes as this on that account.

"Now the first aid work!" commanded the photographer from the opposite shore. The creek was not so wide but what everything taking place on the opposite bank could be clearly seen, while talk could easily be heard. "Work her arms up and down over her head," went on the directing photographer. "Then in about ten seconds signal for the others to come out. Are they all ready, C. C.?"

"Yes, but I guess they've got cramps from

standing so long," replied the gloomy rescuer. "I
know I'll have a cold that——"

"Keep quiet!" came the command. "Your face
is turned this way, now, and your lips show."

"Oh, such a job!" exclaimed the other, in
gloomy despair. "You can't even speak your
mind."

"That's right—speak your lines," said the photographer. "Get ready now. I'll want the others
in a few seconds. I guess——"

But he did not finish. He was interrupted by a
crash that came from the roadway, just beyond
the clump of trees under which the little drama
was being enacted. At this point the road came
close to the creek, and, through an opening in
the bushes and trees, a clear view of the highway
could be had.

Joe and Blake, as well as the photographer,
looked across at the sound of the crash, and saw
a big touring car smash sidewise into a carriage
in which was seated an elderly lady. There was
a splintering of wood, and a rending of metal.
One of the forward mudguards of the auto was
torn off, and left to trail in the dirt. The carriage was tilted at a dangerous angle, one wheel
being broken, and the lady in it was tossed out.
But, fortunately, the horses did not run away, the
colored driver managing to hold them.

Then, without pausing an instant, the reckless motorist put on full speed and dashed away, his mudguard clanging in the dirt and whirling up clouds of dust.

"Look at that!" cried Joe.

"It's Mrs. Randolph!" gasped Blake. "Maybe she's badly hurt. Let's go and see!"

"Just my luck!" cried the photographer. "That smash-up got on the last end of this film, and it'll spoil the picture!"

"Come on!" yelled Blake to Joe. "We'll cross by the bridge and see if we can help her."

CHAPTER III

THE REWARD

"SAY, things are surely happening to us to-day!" exclaimed Joe, as he and his chum ran a little way down the bank of the creek, to where there was a bridge.

"I should say yes," agreed his chum. "I do hope Mrs. Randolph isn't hurt. She was very kind to me when I was sick."

"That's right," went on Joe. "And when she saw me in a ragged suit once she gave me one that had belonged to her son, who died. I was glad to get it, too. She must have slathers of money!"

"She has," agreed Blake, "and no near relatives to leave it to in case she dies."

"We'll hope she won't die," panted Joe, as they raced across the bridge to the aid of Mrs. Betty Randolph, a Southern lady, who had made her home in the town for several years, though originally from Fairfax county, Virginia. She was reputed to be very wealthy, and lived in a fine house. Every fair day she went for a drive behind her fine team, in charge of the old colored man.

And, while I have the opportunity, I will just briefly tell you a little something more about the two boys.

Blake Stewart was an orphan, his father and mother having died some years before this story opens. He was an only child, and when matters were settled up it was found that there was not enough property to provide for him. His mother's brother, Jonathan Haverstraw, who had a small farm in Fayetteburg, in the central part of New York State, offered to take the friendless boy and care for him.

"He can work on the farm with me, when he gets big enough," said Mr. Haverstraw. "I'll do the best I can by him, but it won't be much, for I haven't any means except a small pension, and I'm getting too old to farm it much longer."

So Blake had come to live with his uncle, and he was well treated, though of late he had had to do most of the work on the farm himself, his uncle being in feeble health. But it was not too burdensome, for gradually Mr. Haverstraw gave up crop after crop, being unable to properly sow or harvest them, and not being able to hire help.

A little corn, some potatoes and a vegetable garden was about all under cultivation now, and even that would soon be given up. From what he managed to sell from the garden, and by disposing of eggs and chickens, adding thereto his small pension, Mr. Haverstraw just managed to keep his nephew and himself.

Some two years before this story opens there had come to the town of Fayetteburg a rather ragged lad with a bright and pleasant face, and merry blue eyes that sparkled in spite of the trouble they showed. He applied for work at several farms, telling a straight story. He said he had lost track of his parents, that he was all alone in the world, as far as he knew, and, rather than take a place in a city factory, he had come to the country. His lungs were weak, he said.

But no one needed a boy, especially a feeble one, until the lad applied to Zachariah Bradley, who kept a small place near that of Mr. Haverstraw. To the surprise of nearly every one, Mr. Bradley hired Joe Duncan, which was the new lad's name. It developed that the boy had agreed to work for his board and clothes for several years, and perhaps that influenced Mr. Bradley.

At any rate, Joe came to work for him, and soon the new lad and Blake Stewart became fast chums and friends. Their liking grew with their years, and what little time they had off they spent together. But now new trouble had come to Joe. He had been told that his employer could no longer afford to keep him, for during the past six months Joe had been getting wages.

Not large, of course, only five dollars a month; but he was worth that and more, only Mr. Bradley could not afford to increase it. Now even that small sum was found by the farmer to be too much of a drain on him, and he had notified Joe that he would have to go—or stay and work for nothing, which the lad did not care to do, as he was now much improved in health and stronger.

And, as Joe raced along with Blake toward the scene of the accident, the hired boy was wondering what he was going to do in the next few days—being without a place.

"She's getting up!" exclaimed Blake, referring to Mrs. Randolph, for they now had a clear view of the wrecked carriage. "I guess she can't be badly hurt."

"I hope not," remarked Joe. "But she's limping."

"So she is," agreed Blake. "George, her coachman, seems to be paying more attention to the horses than to his mistress."

"Probably Mrs. Randolph told him to. She thinks a lot of those animals—more than she does of herself, I've heard."

"There come some of the theatrical people, I guess," went on Blake, as he saw several persons coming from the direction of the rescue scene beneath the trees. "They can help the widow if need be."

"One of 'em is that funny man who pulled the lady out," commented Joe. "He's a regular calamity-howler, from the way he talks."

"That's right. Are you hurt, Mrs. Randolph?" the lad asked, eagerly, as he and his chum neared the scene of the smashup. "We saw the accident. Can we help you?"

"Ah! It's Blake Stewart!" exclaimed Mrs. Randolph, in her soft Southern accent; yet, withal, she had a masterful tone.

"Shall we run for a doctor?" put in Joe.

"And here's Joe Duncan!" went on the elderly lady, who was rather a stickler for forms. "I am very glad to see you, boys."

"Can we help you?" persisted Blake.

"Perhaps you can, if you saw that accident!" she exclaimed, somewhat sternly, as she limped nearer to them. "Are the horses much hurt, George?"

"No'm, Miss Randoph. Dey ain't hurted

much. Baby hab a suah 'nuff scratch on her nigh
fo' laig, an' Prince am some cut, but it ain't nuffin
skeerious laik, Miss Randolph!"

"The careless—criminally careless creature!"
exclaimed the elderly widow. "I'll have the law
on him for this, or my name is not Betty Randolph! I'll show him what it means to insult a
Southern lady!"

"But don't you need a doctor?" asked Blake.

"No, I'm all right—just a sprained ankle,"
said Mrs. Randolph. "I'm rather spry yet, in
spite of my age, and I jumped when I heard the
crash. I'm not much hurt, but I'm sorry about
the horses," and she proceeded to examine the
animals, that had been calmed and kept well in
hand by George.

"You say you boys saw this?" she went on,
looking rather curiously at the group of moving
picture actors and actresses who had gathered
about. There were half a dozen in the company.

"Why, yes, we saw it from across the creek,"
spoke Joe.

"And do you think you would know this autoist
again if you should see him?" asked Mrs. Randolph.

"I think so," spoke Blake. "The sun was shin-
ing right on his face, and I had a good look. It
isn't so far from here to where we were."

"I'd know him, too," declared Joe.

"Good!" exclaimed the Southern lady. "If you'll find him and cause his arrest I'll pay you a reward of fifty dollars."

"Fifty dollars!" gasped Joe.

"Yes! Oh, don't look frightened. I can afford it, but I don't intend to spend it out of my own pocket—or, at least, I'll get it back if I do. I'll sue that man for more damages than that! The idea of racing around the country in one of those lawless machines, and smashing my carriage. I'll sue him if it takes my last penny! I'll show him what a Southern lady can do. And I'll pay you boys a reward of fifty dollars if you can find this man for me. Will you do it? My horses alone are easily worth four times that amount to me, to say nothing of my carriage. Will you try to find him for me?"

CHAPTER IV

A STRANGE OFFER

For a moment or two neither Joe nor Blake replied. They did not know what to say, and, coupled with their youth, was the fact that they both faced a change of circumstances. I have not yet told what Blake's was to be, but it will presently develop.

"Well?" asked Mrs. Randolph. "Are you afraid you won't know the man again?"

"No," answered Blake. "I think I could recognize him anywhere."

"And I can help out, if it comes to a pinch," spoke another voice. It was that of the moving picture operator. Mrs. Randolph looked at him in some surprise.

"Who are you, if I may ask?" she said, in her rather stately tones.

"My name is Calvert Hadley, madam," he replied, with a low bow, for he recognized the peculiar attitude of the proud Southern woman.

"Ha! Are you any relation to the Linnberg

Hadleys of Fairfax county, sir?"

"My father was of that family," replied the moving picture operator.

"Ah, I am glad indeed to know that. They were among my closest friends, though I do not remember your father."

"He left the South when but a boy."

"Ah, that accounts for it, then. But I am glad to meet you. I want to shake hands with you," and she performed the ceremony with stately grace. "You say you can aid these boys in identifying this man—whoever he was—who was so criminally careless?" she asked.

"Yes. As it happened, I was taking some moving pictures for the Film Theatrical Company, by which I am employed. The scene—a rescue from the creek—was almost over, when your carriage came in range of the camera. That would not have so much mattered, for its appearance would not have detracted from the rescue, but when the smash came it was too vivid to fit in with the bringing back to life of a supposedly drowned person. I shall have to cut that part of the film out and do part of the act over again."

"I am sorry to cause you any trouble, Mr. Hadley."

"Oh, it was not your fault, madam, I assure you," and again the photographer bowed low.

Evidently he knew what was expected toward a stately Southern dame.

"I am glad to hear you say that," went on Mrs. Randolph; "for I may need your evidence when I sue him—that is, if these boys can locate him for me. But you say you can help them?"

"Yes, Mrs. Randolph."

"How?"

"Why, as it happened, I was exposing the film when the accident happened. Every detail of it will come out clearly, as it was in the bright sunlight. The face of the autoist was right in focus, and it will be an easy matter to reproduce a photo of it, or project it in large size on a screen. Of course, as soon as I saw the accident, I stopped the camera, so I only have a few views of it."

"I am glad of it—in a way," said the Southern lady, with a smile; "for I should not care to win fame by being depicted in a moving picture play; and friends of Betty Randolph would doubtless be astonished to see her likeness thrown on a screen, showing her leaping from a wrecked carriage. But I am glad you have that man's picture. Now, boys, will you try for the reward?"

"I fancy we'd all like to try, madam," put in the man who had performed the "rescue."

Mrs. Randolph turned to look at him, and became aware of his water-soaked condition.

"Ah—er—I don't believe—why, good gracious, man!" she exclaimed, with a change of manner. "You are all wet! What happened? You must get dry clothes at once! Get into my carriage, and George——"

"Yes'm, Miss Randolph!"

"Oh, I forgot; my carriage is smashed. But this gentleman ought to be looked after."

"Oh, don't worry about me, madam," put in "C. C.," as Joe and Blake had begun to call him. "I'm used to this sort of thing. I suppose I shall catch my death of cold, but it is all in the interests of science."

"He jumped in to rescue the lady," explained Joe.

"Rescue the lady!" exclaimed Mrs. Randolph. "Where is the poor creature? Sir, I wish to shake your hand! Rescued a lady, that is——"

"It was the moving picture play," explained Mr. Hadley, quickly. "It was only acting, Mrs. Randolph."

"Oh!" she exclaimed. "I'm afraid I'm a little bit behind the times. I used to be a patron of the drama, and many times have I seen the elder Booth. But to jump in water to rescue a lady merely to make a picture—well, I confess it is beyond me. But then, I'm old-fashioned, I fear. Now I must find some way of getting home, and you boys—I declare it takes you a good while to make up your minds," and she smiled at Joe and Blake, for she knew them both well, and had often befriended them. "Will you try for that reward, or not?"

"I'm willing to!" exclaimed Blake, quickly.

"And so am I!" added his chum; "though I don't know how in the world we can find that man."

"He must be found!" said Mrs. Randolph, firmly. "I intend suing him for damages. I want him found."

"Perhaps I can help you, boys," said Mr. Hadley, in a low voice to the lads. "I'll talk to you in a little while."

The members of the theatrical company crowded around Mrs. Randolph, offering assistance, and one of the young ladies, whom Blake thought extremely pretty, pinned up a rent in the dress of the victim of the accident.

"I shall be all right, and thank you all very much," said Mrs. Randolph, after a pause. "I must get to my home now. Boys, come to me as soon as you have this careless autoist arrested—or even located—and I will attend to the rest; or, rather, my lawyer will. Now, George, do you think you could borrow a carriage somewhere, and take me home?"

"Yes'm, Miss Randolph. I suah can do dat. Anybody around heah gwine t' lend us a keeridge."

"Well, get somebody, not anybody, George," ordered his mistress. "And you had better arrange to leave the team in some stable here, so as not to lame them by driving them after they have been cut and bruised."

"You might get a carriage at Mr. Henderson's," suggested Joe, and when the colored man departed in the direction of a nearby farmhouse, this was proven to be so, for he presently came back with a rather dilapidated rig, for which Mr. Henderson apologized.

"It doesn't matter," said Mrs. Randolph, graciously. "I am greatly obliged to you. I'll send the wheelwright out to get my carriage, and the veterinarian will look after my team. Thank you all, very much. You boys, don't forget that you are to find that man for me!

"Why, such reckless conduct I never heard of! I was driving peaceably along, on the right side of the highway, when I heard the toot of the horn behind me. I even told George to turn out still more to avoid any possible accident, for I can't bear those dust-raising machines. Then he crashed into me without any excuse whatever."

"That's right, Mrs. Randolph," declared Joe.

"And he drove off without even stopping to inquire if I was hurt!" went on the indignant lady. "That will be a point against him when I bring suit, I fancy."

"Indeed, it will," agreed **Mr. Hadley.**

By this time Mrs. Randolph was ready to drive on, and after good-byes to those who had gathered about her, and with renewed admonitions to the boys to keep on the trail of the reckless autoist, she left.

"Well," said Mr. Hadley, suggestively, after a pause; "I guess we'd better finish up that act, and then get back to the city and arrange for the scenes there. I'll have to slip in a new reel, though. The tag end of the first one was spoiled by that accident, though if I'd known it was going to be pulled off I could have gotten a dandy picture of it."

"Have I got to go through all that rescue business again?" asked the actor who had leaped into the creek. "If I have, I'm going to quit. I'm all wet now, and I'm sure I'm getting the snifflers," and then he did a funny little dance, and sang a snatch of a comic song that seemed to prove him in good spirits, in spite of his doleful words.

"Oh, cut it, Gloomy," suggested a tall, dark-complexioned man who, it afterward appeared, was the "leading heavy," or the villain, in the picture dramas.

"You won't have to do much more, C. C.," spoke Mr. Hadley. "Just the reviving business, and then the others will come on the 'stage,' and carry Miss Shay off. That will end this part of it. The next act takes place in Syracuse."

"Good! Back to civilization!" exclaimed the gloomy actor, who, it appeared, seemed to look for trouble everywhere. "I know we'll never get anything to eat here."

"Say, aren't you afraid it's going to snow?" sarcastically asked the youngest of the two ladies in the company, the one whom Blake had thought so pretty. "It looks like frost," she added, glancing at the bright and warm sunlight.

"It may rain before night," conceded the actor. "But let's get it over with."

The little company of actors and actresses took their way to the bank of the stream, and Joe and Blake followed, crossing the bridge, for they were more interested in seeing the moving picture machine work than in the drama itself, though, from their vantage point, they could observe it.

"Isn't it great!" exclaimed Joe, enthusiastically.

"It sure is," agreed his chum, for the third or fourth time that day.

Little time was lost in putting a new reel of

films in the machine, and then the resuscitating part of the act was gone through with again. At the right moment the rest of the company poured from behind the screening trees, in answer to simulated signals for aid made by the actor who had made the "rescue," and the act was over.

"Now for Syracuse!" exclaimed Mr. Hadley, as he began packing his machine, while the boys looked on. "You see," he continued, "we're from New York, but there's one play we have to make pictures for that is laid in Syracuse. So we had to come up here to get views, and as one of them is supposed to take place on the banks of a stream, we came out here. It was more convenient, and a crowd was less likely to gather."

"You said you might be able to help us identify that autoist," suggested Blake.

"That's right, so I did. Well, what I was going to say was this: The end of the film, with the accident scene on it, is of no use to me. I've got to cut it off and fasten this part on that I just took. Now you can have those accident pictures if you like, and properly enlarged, they'll give you a good view of that scoundrel's face. He ought to be arrested for reckless driving, and be made to pay heavy damages. So if you want to take a chance on the reward I'll be glad to help you."

"I'd like to," said Joe.

"And we'll be much obliged for that film," added Blake.

"All right. I'll have it developed and some pictures printed from it, and send them to you," went on Mr. Hadley. "How do you think you'd like this sort of work?" he asked, with a smile.

"It's great!" declared Joe. "But I'd like to see some of the finished pictures, too."

"So would I," added Blake.

"Now I'll tell you something that's been on my mind for the last half hour," went on the photographer; "ever since, in fact, I had to keep you from jumping in to spoil my picture. I need a couple of bright boys for a new line of work I'm thinking of taking up in connection with these films. How would you like to become moving picture boys?"

For a moment neither answered, and then Joe, who had been wondering what was to become of him, exclaimed:

"I'll jump at the chance!"

Then, somewhat to his surprise, Blake added: "And so will I."

CHAPTER V

BLAKE EXPLAINS

Joe Duncan could hardly repress an exclamation of astonishment at Blake's words.

"Why, Blake!" he said. "You don't mean to say you are going to leave your uncle, and start off on a new job? In my case it's different. My job left me before I left it, and I just had to get something else to do. Mr. Hadley's offer came just in time. But you've got a good place with your uncle, and——"

"That's just the point!" exclaimed Blake, smiling slightly. "I haven't got it."

"What's that?" cried Joe.

"It's just as I say," went on Blake. "I can't stay at my uncle's place after this week, so I'm just as badly off as you are."

"And you've got to get out and hustle just as I have?"

"That's it, Joe, and I'm just as much pleased over this offer as you are. I only hope we can make good."

38

"Oh, I'm sure you can fill the bill," spoke the moving picture man, with a smile. "I'm pretty good at reading characters, and I have yours down pat, I believe. I think you'll be just what I need. But it is rather surprising to find both you boys under the necessity of looking for places at the same time. You're chums, I take it?"

"That's right," said Joe. "But this is the first I knew that Blake was about to lose his place. What's the trouble?"

"I'll tell you," volunteered Blake. "You remember a while back, just before we came fishing, I started to say something and stopped?"

Joe nodded.

"Well, I was going to tell you then that I would soon be obliged to leave my uncle's farm," resumed Blake, "but I decided to postpone the bad news. This is how it came about: My uncle is getting old and feeble, as I guess you know, Joe. He can hardly work the small amount of ground we now have under cultivation, and that means that he'd have to hire a man, for I'm not equal to it. We talked it over the other night— he and I—and he decided to give up the farm."

"Give up the farm!" exclaimed Joe. "Why, he owns it, doesn't he?"

"Yes, but it isn't worth much and is heavily mortgaged. He has a fairly good offer for it, so he is going to close it up next week. That means I'm out of a place."

"But where is your uncle going?" asked Mr. Hadley, as he continued to pack up his moving picture apparatus. The rest of the company had gone to the Fayetteburg Hotel, where they would change their garments and proceed to Syracuse. "It seems to me," resumed the photographer, "that if your uncle has been providing for you, and if he is going to sell his farm, and get cash, he ought to continue to look after you.

"Mind you!" he exclaimed. "I want you to come with me, for I think I can advance you, and I know there is a good opening in this field for a bright young chap—or, for that matter, two of them.

"But at the same time, I don't want to take an unfair advantage of you. If you have a fairly wealthy relative, perhaps it would be better to remain with him, though I want you to understand that my offer still holds good."

"I'm glad it does," said Blake, "because I'm going to accept it. I haven't finished explaining. After my uncle decided to sell his farm, he went further and made up his mind that as he could not expect to get any younger or stronger, he would do better to enter some home for the aged. And that is what he is going to do. By paying in a certain lump sum, that will take about all he gets for the sale of his farm, he is guaranteed a home for life. That, with his little pension, will make him sure of being cared for in his old age."

"And that means you have to leave?" asked Joe.

"That's it," went on Blake. "I can't go to the home with him, and the man who has bought the farm says he doesn't need my valuable assistance," and Blake laughed.

"In that case, come with me!" exclaimed the photographer. "As long as you are both alone in the world, you can't do any worse, and, while I can't guarantee that you'll become millionaires, or even rich, still there are good chances.

"The moving picture business has advanced by leaps and bounds in the past few years, and it is still going. Some men have made fortunes out of it, and thousands in it are making a good, comfortable living. The amusement end isn't all there is to it, though that's the end most persons see. It will not be long before the educational features will be made more of than they are to-day. That line is capable of wide enlargement and it is going to be taken advantage of. Schools and colleges are going to use moving picture machines in place of some text-books soon, and the pupils will gain knowledge easier and better.

"There!" he exclaimed, with a laugh, "I didn't mean to deliver such a lecture, but I'm very much interested in this sort of work, and I know there's a big future in it. Who knows—perhaps you boys may even rival Mr. Edison, who is credited with having made the first commercial appliance to show pictures in natural movement, though if he had not had the celluloid films to use, probably he would not have succeeded. So you see there is a big chance for you boys."

"This is interesting!" exclaimed Blake. "There must be quite a history to moving pictures, Mr. Hadley."

"There is, boys, and it is history that is still being written."

"Can you tell us something about it?" asked Joe.

"Yes, but I haven't the time now. If you boys really decide to come with me, I'll arrange to meet you in New York, and then I can not only tell you something of the business, but I can show you as well.

"The concern I am with—the Film Theatrical Company—maintains a regular theatre for making photo plays, as well as a road company, and in addition we get all sorts of other interesting views."

"That sounds good!" exclaimed Joe. "I

wouldn't miss this for a whole lot. So, Blake, you're going to quit farming, the same as I am?"

"Yes, I've got to. As I said, the man who takes my uncle's place doesn't need my help."

"Have you no other relatives who might look after you?" asked the photographer. "Mind, I'm only saying this so as not to take an unfair advantage of you," he explained.

"No other relatives," replied Blake. "And, if I had, I don't believe I'd go to them. I'd rather make my own way in the world, as long as I have a chance."

"And I'll give you the chance," declared the picture man. "Now, as to arrangements. I have to go on to Syracuse with the company to-night. We expect to be in New York the first of next week. Do you boys think you could make your way there, and find me?"

"I guess so," answered Blake. "Though I've never had much chance to travel."

"Me either," said Joe.

"Well, if things go right, you'll have all the travel you want," said Mr. Hadley. "I mentioned to you that I had plans in mind for a new feature of this picture business—that is, not exactly new, but an extension of the branch that is now rather neglected. I can't give you details yet, but I will soon. Now here is the address of

our concern, and you can find me there almost
any time.   It's printed on this card—I'll give
you each one—and when you arrive in New York
any policeman can tell you how to get there.
Here is money for your traveling expenses," and
he produced a roll of bills.

"Oh, I don't want that!" exclaimed Blake,
drawing back. "I've got a little cash, and my
uncle is going to give me a hundred dollars when
he sells the farm."

"And I've got about thirty-five dollars saved
up," declared Joe, proudly. "It took some saving,
too, let me tell you!"

"That's all right," went on the photographer,
good-naturedly. "I'm glad to know that you
boys appreciate the value of money. At the same
time, this is business with me. We always pay
traveling expenses, and there's no reason why
you should be excepted from the rule. Besides,
you'll find when you get to New York, that it's
a pretty expensive place to live in, even half-way
decently. So take this cash—it doesn't come out
of my pocket; the firm supplies it, and the head
of it, Mr. Jacob Ringold, told me to be on the
lookout for a couple of bright boys. I don't need
to look any further, for I've found 'em, I guess,"
and he smiled at the two lads.

"Much obliged," said Joe.

"Would you mind," said Blake, "as long as you're telling us something about the company, to say why you call that one man C. C.?"

"Oh, you mean Gloomy!" said the photographer, with a laugh. "Well, he is a case. He's our comedian, you know, though he sometimes fills other roles. And, like a number of funny men, including clowns, he's gloomy in private life, though the drollest fellow imaginable when acting. He is always on the lookout for trouble."

"We noticed that," said Joe, with a smile.

"But what's his name?" asked Blake.

"His name is Christopher Cutler Piper, but we always speak of him as C. C., those letters being the initials of his first two names. When we don't call him Gloomy, we call him C. C."

"C. C.," mused Blake. "What an odd name!"

"It's his own doing," declared Mr. Hadley. "I believe when he was young the boys used to call him Christopher Custard, instead of Christopher Cutler, and he got so out of patience that, ever after, he only used his initials—C. C."

By this time the photographer had put away his various pieces of apparatus. Joe and Blake had picked up their fishpoles, but all desire to cast in had now left them. Their minds were too filled with new, big ideas.

"Then it's all settled," said Mr. Hadley, as he

started back for the hotel, in a carriage he had hired. "You'll meet me in New York next week?"

"We will!" cried Joe and Blake.

CHAPTER VI

READY TO START

LEFT to themselves, with the photographer driving off, the two youths stood and looked at each other for several seconds without saying a word. Then Blake exclaimed

"I can hardly believe it!"

"Me either," added his chum. "Here a little while ago I was looking for work, and feeling pretty bad because I didn't seem able to find any. Now I've got the prospect of a fine position, and in New York, of all places in the world! I've always wanted to go there."

"So have I," said Blake. "And in my case, too, there's been a big change in a few hours. I was feeling pretty badly about leaving Uncle Jonathan; but now, on the whole, I'm glad of it.

"There never would have been much of a future here," he went on; "and I never cared much for farm work. Then, too, Uncle Jonathan will be better off in the home, for he's getting too old to work hard. Yes, I guess it's a good thing all around that we met this theatrical party."

"But I wonder what sort of work he's going to have us do?" mused Joe. "He didn't tell us exactly."

"No, he doesn't seem to have all his plans made yet. But of course it has something to do with moving pictures, and there's a big future in almost any branch of that business. I'm sure it will just suit me."

"So am I; but say, Blake, what about trying for that reward Mrs. Randolph offered? Are you going to do that if we go to New York?"

"Well, I don't see how we can, very well, and yet we passed our words. That autoist might be a tourist who lives in New York. He had a big and powerful car, such as I imagine those millionaire New Yorkers usually own. We might accidentally run across him in the big city."

"As long as he doesn't run across us it will be all right," laughed Joe. "But I guess it's as you say. We said we'd try to locate him, and we will. Cracky! It would be great if we could collect that reward."

"That's so," agreed Blake. "Say, I've got an idea."

"What is it?"

"Why, you noticed, didn't you, that the mud-guard on the car was broken in the smashup?"

"Sure I did. It was dragging on the ground."

"Well, my idea is that if we make some inquiries in the village we might get on the track of this fellow. Folks are sure to have noticed him, racing along with his mudguard dangling. They can tell us what direction he took, and he may even have stopped at the blacksmith shop to have it fixed."

"He'd hardly do that, knowing he might be chased," objected Joe.

"Oh, I don't know," was Blake's opinion. "Some of those reckless autoists take lots of chances. He might have figured that he could get the guard fixed, and race off again before word of the accident reached town. Besides, it would be dangerous to travel with that piece dragging, and it attracts notice."

"That's right," agreed Joe. "We'll make some inquiries."

"And then we'll have to tell about our new jobs," added Blake. "I guess Uncle Jonathan will be glad I have a place."

"And Mr. Bradley won't care whether I go or stay," said Joe, referring to his employer. "He was kind enough in his way," he continued, "but he was too poor to pay me decent wages. I'm going to work hard when I get to New York, and see if I can't get rich."

"The same here!" cried Blake. "We won't be the first to have made a fortune out of the moving picture business."

The boys tramped over the fields, and soon came to the country road that led to the two farms where they were employed. Joe reached his place first, and, arranging to meet Blake a little later and go to the village to make inquiries, he went in the house.

As Joe had anticipated, his employer evinced little interest in the lad's change of fortune. Mr. Bradley said he was glad the lad had found a place.

"But New York's an awful wicked city," he warned. "You want to be on the lookout for thieves all the while. They'll get your money, sure."

"I won't have an awful lot after I pay a couple of weeks' board," laughed Joe. "I suppose I can stay here with you until I get ready to go?"

"You can—if you want to pay your board," was the cautious answer.

Joe felt a little disappointed at this. He certainly thought he had done enough for Mr. Bradley for nothing to be allowed to remain a few days for the sake of the additional work he would do; but Mrs. Bradley, as well as her husband, had the name of being "close."

"All right; I'll think about it," said Joe. "I may stay at the hotel," and he walked off to do some of the chores.

"I'll give you as good food as you'll get at the hotel," said Mrs. Bradley, quickly. "I'd board you for nothing, Joe, but we can't afford it. Mr. Bradley broke a hoe handle a little while ago, and it'll cost as much as thirty-five cents for a new one. Otherwise I wouldn't charge you anything; but, as it is, I'll have to."

"All right," answered Joe. Somehow the matter did not worry him as it would have done a few hours before. He had, as I have said, some money saved up, and the prospect of work cheered him very much.

Blake's uncle was surprised, and, on the whole, rather delighted at the prospects of his nephew.

"I'm glad to hear you have a chance," he said. "It will make me worry less after I retire and go to live in the home. I have been puzzling my brains trying to think of a way to provide for you, but I couldn't seem to hit on any plan. And now it has solved itself. New York is a wonderful city. I was there when a young man, but it must have changed a lot since. There will be many opportunities, and, though I don't know anything about these moving pictures, it sounds like a nice, clean business, and I hope you make a success of it—you and Joe. It's a great thing to be young," and the aged man, who was nearing the end of his term of life, sighed heavily.

However, he did not want to make Blake feel gloomy, so, brightening up, he asked many questions about what happened that afternoon, and how the chance had come to his nephew.

"Fifty dollars reward, eh?" he exclaimed, as he heard of the auto accident. "I'm sure I hope you get it. It's a lot of money; but then, Mrs. Randolph is rich. I hope you get the fellow."

"If I do I'll have to get more of a hustle on than this," declared Blake, with a laugh, as he finished some work around the barn. "I guess I'll call for Joe now, and we'll see if we can learn anything."

However, he did not have to go for his chum, for a few minutes later the farm boy arrived, ready to proceed down to the village. It did not require much in the way of inquiry to learn something of the reckless autoist.

Word of the accident to Mrs. Randolph had spread rapidly, and when the boys reached the centre of the town they found a number of persons who had seen the big car rush through the village at racing speed.

"And the mudguard was dangling and banging away on the road like a house afire!" exclaimed Jared Sprintz, one of the constables. "I had some notion of arrestin' him, only 'fore I had a chance to figger out how I was goin' to do it, he was out of sight and nigh on to Bradford township, I guess."

"Not much chance for us to catch him," decided Blake, as he and Joe listened to different versions of the speed at which the unknown had been traveling.

"No," agreed Joe. "We'll wait until we get those pictures from Mr. Hadley. They may help some."

"If we had the number of the auto we could easily find out who owns it," said Blake. "Each machine is recorded, you know."

"That's right!" exclaimed Joe. "I wonder if we could?"

But, on inquiry, it was found that while several persons had noticed the number on the big car, no two individuals gave the same figures, and of course it was out of the question to proceed with the identification on that score.

"Well, we'll keep our eyes open," decided Blake, as he and his chum started back toward their houses as dusk was falling. "I haven't much to do from now until we leave for New

York, and maybe I'll take some trips around the country on that old bicycle that looks as if it came over in the Mayflower," for he had, some time before, gotten possession of a second-hand wheel, which he had managed to fix up to do fair service.

"Well, I'm going to take a sort of a vacation myself," declared Joe. "If I've got to pay board, I'm not going to work."

"Pay board!" exclaimed Blake.

"Yes," answered Joe, and he told of the farmer's plan.

"Oh, say, that's a shame!" exclaimed his chum. "Say, look here! You come and stay with me until it's time to leave for New York. I'm sure my uncle will be glad to have you, and while we don't live high, I guess we can feed you as well as Mrs. Bradley could. Come ahead. You and I'll have lots to talk over, anyhow."

"Oh, I don't know——" began Joe.

"Yes, you will!" exclaimed Blake, decidedly. "You've got to come." And so it was arranged. That night Joe said good-by to the farmer for whom he had worked several years, and transferred his clothes to the house of Blake's uncle, who welcomed his nephew's chum warmly.

The boys quickly made their preparations to go to New York. They did not have many belongings, though their clothing was good, if not of the best materials. Mr. Haverstraw continued his arrangements for disposing of the farm and entering the home. He gave Blake the money he had promised, and with nearly one hundred and fifty dollars between them the boys did not feel exactly poor as they got ready to leave. They had made several inquiries about the autoist in the days that followed the accident, but aside from word that he had been seen passing through this or that town nothing definite was learned. Then Mrs. Randolph increased the reward from fifty to one hundred dollars.

"I guess we'll never get that reward," said Joe, in hopeless tones, when he heard of the increase.

"Oh, wait until we get to New York," said Blake. "We may meet that rascal face to face unexpectedly. I hope we do."

"If we do, I'll grab him and yell for the police!" declared Joe, with a laugh.

They were anxiously waiting word from Mr. Hadley as to when they were to start, when one afternoon, about a week following the accident and the scenes at the moving picture demonstration, Blake got a bulky letter from the post-office.

"It's from New York!" he cried to Joe, who was with him. "I guess it's the pictures of that autoist!"

CHAPTER VII

IN THE BIG CITY

BLAKE's guess proved correct, for, on opening the envelope, there came to light a number of enlarged photographs, and a letter, a glance at the signature to which showed it to be from Mr. Hadley.

"Hurray!" cried Blake, when he had glanced over the communication. "He wants us to come on as soon as we can. He says his new, big idea is all ready to spring, and he wants our help."

"Does he say what the idea is?" asked Joe.

"No; he says he'll tell us when he sees us."

"What about the clue pictures?"

"These are the ones he promised us—part of the film that was nearly spoiled by the accident," went on the other lad, as he read further along in the letter.

"He says he cut off the end of the film," went on Blake; "and had some enlargements of the man's face made. He says he hopes we catch him, but he doesn't think we will. But say, Joe,

56

that face is as plain as can be," and he held out one of the photographs. "If we ever see him in real life, we'll know him."

"That's right," agreed the other lad; "and look! you can see Mrs. Randolph standing by the broken carriage."

"Yes, and the coachman, George, too. Say, those moving picture cameras must be wonderful machines."

"I guess they are. We'll soon know more about 'em, for Mr. Hadley seems to understand them from the ground up. What about going to New York?"

"We can start any time we like, the letter says. We're to let him know what day we'll come, and are to go right to the address he gave us. He'll meet us there, and arrange for a boarding place. I wish I knew what sort of work we were going to do, though."

"So do I. It must be something about moving pictures, however. Maybe he wants us to pose, or maybe take some views."

"We haven't had experience enough," objected Blake. "But we'll soon know what it is. I don't see why we can't leave for New York day after to-morrow."

"I guess we can. I'm ready."

"Then we'll plan that, and drop Mr. Hadley a line," which they did before returning home.

Even with the enlarged pictures of the reckless autoist, the boys were no nearer finding him than they were before. They spent time making inquiries about the country, hoping perhaps the man might be touring back that way, but they got no trace of him.

Their final arrangements were made, and they were all packed up one night, ready to start for New York in the morning, when they were surprised to receive a call from Mrs. Randolph.

"What's this I hear about you boys?" she asked. "Going to New York, and into the moving picture business?"

"That's right," said Blake.

"Well, what about finding that reckless man for me?" went on the Southern lady, with a smile. "One of my horses was hurt worse than I thought at first, and I'm determined to make that fellow pay the damages. I'll teach him that we Southern women know how to take care of ourselves. I hope you boys aren't going to forget about that quest. I'm still in earnest about it, and I am going to increase the reward to two hundred dollars."

"Oh, we're not going to give up," declared Joe.

"Maybe we can pick him up in New York. If we do we can let you know."

"I wish you would," went on the lady. "Of course I could hire private detectives to do this work, I suppose, but I do not like the idea. Perhaps I am too sanguine in trusting you boys— some of my friends have said so—but I don't believe I am. I have faith in you."

"We'll do our best," said Blake, as he explained what had already been done; "but it isn't going to be easy."

"I realize that," spoke Mrs. Randolph, "and I am going to help you all I can. I have started suit against this man—whoever he may be— under the name of John Doe, which is always done when you don't know a person's real name. My lawyer has gotten some kind of paper from the court, and here it is for you."

"Why, it's something like a warrant," exclaimed Blake, as he examined it.

"Very likely," said the Southern lady. "I know very little about such things. My lawyer attends to it all, but he said that would be honored anywhere, and that if the man could be found, any officer would be justified in arresting him, once he was shown that paper."

"This will be just what we need, in case we find that fellow!" exclaimed Joe.

"That's right," agreed Blake, and then, after their visitor had been told their plans, she departed.

There was little more to do for the lads to get ready. Early the next morning they were on their way, having said good-by to their few friends in the village. Mr. Haverstraw was to go to the Home for the Aged that afternoon, his farm being taken possession of by the man to whom he had sold it, who would also use the house and contents just as they stood.

"Well, we're off!" remarked Joe, as their train pulled out of the Syracuse station, they having gone there to get a through express.

"That's right!" agreed Blake. "We've got the whole world before us."

"A moving picture world," added Joe.

Their journey would take most of the day, and they settled themselves comfortably. Little of incident occurred, but the boys thoroughly enjoyed the trip, for never before had they taken such a long one. In due time they arrived at the Grand Central Terminal, and found themselves in the metropolis.

"What a busy place!" exclaimed Joe, as he and his chum looked about bewildered, having reached Thirty-third street, near which were located the offices of the Film Theatrical Company. "It makes my head swim!"

"It sure does," agreed Blake. "It's some different from the quiet farm. But let's see which way we're to go. Oh, look at the autos!"

"And trolleys and everything else on wheels!" added Joe, as they marveled at the congestion of traffic. "It's as much as your life is worth to try to get through here."

But their problem was solved for them by a friendly policeman, who, seeing their confusion and "greenness," signaled for them to advance when the line of vehicles had come to a momentary stop. Up to now they had found their way by dint of asking questions, and now Blake, giving the address of Mr. Hadley's place, had it pointed out to him and his chum. They did not have far to go before arriving at the big building, and in an elevator they were shot up to the top story.

"Pretty near the clouds, I should judge," remarked Joe, as they mounted higher and higher.

"Yes, he said they had to be up high, to get all the light they could," explained Blake. "It takes a bright light to make pictures as fast as they have to be taken by the moving cameras."

They entered a door marked "Office," and no sooner were they in than a voice cried:

"Hello, boys! You got here all right. Glad to see you!" and Mr. Hadley rushed out from an inner room, and shook hands with them.

"Just make yourselves at home for half an hour or so, will you? I've got an important stunt on, and I've got to pull it off now. I'll soon be back and take charge of you. Here, C. C., come and show these boys the ropes until I get back. I've got to get that fire scene."

The gloomy comedian came out and smiled at sight of the boys, whom he evidently remembered.

"Come on here, Jack; get my tripod, and rustle out that small camera," directed Mr. Hadley, while C. C. Piper was shaking hands with Joe and Blake. "I want to get those fire pictures before the building burns down."

"You'll never do it," declared Mr. Piper, with gloomy foreboding. "It'll be so hot that your film will melt; or, if that doesn't happen, a hose will burst and spoil everything," and then, as if in contrast, he began humming the latest comic song.

"Cheerful as ever—isn't he, boys?" called the moving picture man, as he hurried out. "If it doesn't rain it'll snow; or, if not, there'll be an earthquake. See you later!" and with the tripod of a camera clutched under his arm, Mr. Hadley made a rush for the elevator.

CHAPTER VIII

THEIR NEW WORK

"HE'LL never get it!" exclaimed C. C., as he and the boys listened to the fast falling footsteps of Mr. Hadley and his helper. "He'll miss that car, sure."

But the clang of the elevator door gave evidence otherwise, and the gloomy comedian said, with a shrug of his shoulders:

"Well, I believe that fire will be out when he gets there, anyhow."

"Why does he want a picture of a fire?" asked Blake, wondering if the actor ever took a rosy view of life.

"Oh, some new stunt he is working up, I believe. But are you boys going to be employed here?"

"I guess so," answered Joe.

"Juvenile leads, heavy, villains or supes?" asked the actor.

"I don't believe we understand you," spoke Blake, with a smile.

"Why, I was just asking what line of acting you were going in for."

"Oh, none at all, I guess," replied Blake. "We haven't been told what our work is going to be, but I think it has to do with the taking of the pictures, and not the posing for them or making them. We don't know how to act."

"Glad to hear you say so," came from the comedian. "I was afraid you might be after my place. Like to watch us at work? We're going to put on the second act of a society drama in a few minutes and it might be interesting to you while waiting for Mr. Hadley to come back."

"We would like to see it," said Joe, and the comedian led them out into a big studio, which was fitted up like a theatre, with much scenery, many "properties" and a number of men and women standing about. In some corners moving picture cameras were clicking and the subjects were going through their acts. The boys were rather surprised to see several scenes being acted at once, each one being photographed separately.

They learned later that this was in the interests of economy and time. As but a small space is required in which to make interior views, it is often possible to make several at the same time, illustrating totally different plays, and often the same set of actors will pass from one scene to another, assuming different characters.

Big electric lights gave additional illumination to the studio theatre, though the glass roof would seem to make it brilliant enough. But, so the boys were told later, such is the speed at which some of the films are worked, the very highest illumination possible is needed.

"Come on, now, get ready there, C. C.!" yelled a voice, and a man, evidently the stage manager, motioned to the gloomy actor. "Get ready with that funny stunt of yours, and make some of those funny faces," he directed, and the comedian who, it appeared, was to take part in a pantomime play, designed to interest children, got on a clown's suit.

"I know something will happen to spoil this film," he said to no one in particular, as he performed some funny antics. "I feel it in my bones."

"Oh, drop that sort of talk, Gloomy," urged the stage manager. "You're always looking for trouble."

"And he has less than any of us," put in another voice. Looking around, Joe and Blake saw Miss Shay, the lady who had fallen out of the boat in the creek that day they had first met. She nodded to the boys, and, crossing the stage, asked them how they liked their first glimpse of New York and the moving picture business.

"Great!" declared Joe and Blake in chorus.

"All ready now!" broke in the stage manager, and while C. C. proceeded to do his funny stunts, other actors and actresses went through a ball-room scene in one section of the studio, while next to them was represented a business office, with a man dictating letters to his stenographer, who, in the person of Birdie Lee, the pretty girl Blake had seen before, clicked away at a typewriter as naturally as if she was actually getting off letters instead of merely posing for pictures.

"Isn't this wonderful?" exclaimed Joe. "To think that we're going to be in this business. We wouldn't have dared dream of it two weeks ago."

"That's right," agreed Blake, looking on interestedly, and trying to gaze in several directions at once. As I intend in following books of this series to tell something of the theatrical end of the moving picture business, I will not go into details of it here, for I have something else in mind. Sufficient to say, for the present, that Joe and Blake were so taken up with watching the acting that they did not note the passage of time. It was not until a voice, speaking to them at their backs, made them turn around, that they were aware Mr. Hadley had returned, and that it was getting dusk, as evidenced by the additional electric lights turned on.

"Well, I'm through for the day," explained the photographer; "and now I'll take you in charge. You must be tired and hungry. I'll take you to a good boarding place I've picked out for you, and you can have supper. Where are your trunk checks?"

They gave them to him and he promised to have their baggage brought from the station by an expressman.

"How do you like it?" he asked, waving his hand toward the animated scenes in front of them.

"Immensely!" exclaimed Blake.

"And even C. C. couldn't scare you off?"

"No; he didn't try very hard," answered Joe, with a laugh. "But did you get your fire scene, and did the hose burst?"

"Yes, I got it all right, and I think it'll make a good film," went on the photographer. "No hose burst, either, and I got some good views of a rescue."

"Is it for a moving picture?" asked Blake.

"That's what it is, and, as I intend to work you into that branch of the business, I might as well explain now as at any other time. Come, we'll walk toward the boarding house and talk on the way.

"Did you boys ever see a moving picture newspaper?" the photographer went on.

"Do you mean one telling about the business, and giving news and printing advertisements of shows?" inquired Joe.

"Not exactly. I mean a series of moving picture films, taken daily, weekly or perhaps monthly, showing current events, such as coronations, inaugurations, and all sorts of events of interest. Just as an ordinary newspaper prints the news of what happens, the moving picture newspaper shows pictures of the same thing."

"I think I have read something about that," said Blake.

"Of course the idea isn't altogether new," said the photographer. "One French firm makes a business of getting views of unusual events all over the world, keeping men in readiness to go North, East, South or West, to snap a volcano in action, or get war views. Now my idea is to do something like that here, only, instead of getting foreign views, I intend to get some showing life in this great city—its perils, its humor and sadness, as well as scenes of ordinary news interest—big buildings going up, industrial occupations, and all that."

"It sounds interesting," declared Joe.

"I'm going to make it interesting," exclaimed

the moving picture man. "There's a big field here, and I've induced Mr. Ringold, the head of this company, to take it up. I'm to have charge of this branch of the business, and I had been thinking of it for some time when I met you boys out there in the country. Of course, I might have gotten some lads here to help me, but I wanted some one whom I could train to work my way, and who would be willing to learn. Lots of city chaps are too filled with ideas of their own importance to do this.

"But I decided to give you a chance, and that's why I had you come on here. I have been given full charge by Mr. Ringold, but one stipulation is that I must make good—that is, I'll have to show that a weekly, or maybe a daily, moving picture newspaper can be made to pay expenses. I must get unusual scenes, and have them timely. It's going to be a hustling job, and there'll be hard work, but I think you'll like it."

"I know we shall!" cried Blake, with sparkling eyes.

"The pay will be good," went on Mr. Hadley, "and I won't work you to death. You will be my assistants in going about from place to place to get the views. I am going to arrange with the fire and police departments to tip us off when anything big happens, so we can get on the ground at once. I am also going to have a news ticker installed, that will give flashes of all sorts of happenings in this vicinity. Now, then, are you ready to become something like reporters on a moving picture newspaper?"

"I am!" cried Joe, and Blake echoed the words.

"Then it's settled," said the photographer. "I'll explain more about it later. This won't be like ordinary moving picture work, for one reel of film, say a thousand feet long, will contain many scenes of different kinds."

"Do you think we'll be able to do what you want?" asked Joe, a bit doubtfully.

"Oh, certainly, after I give you instructions," declared the photographer. "I'll be patient with you. Don't worry. Well, here we are at the boarding house. I live near here myself, so I know the neighborhood is good. And I guess you can eat some supper. I know I can. Come in and I'll introduce you to the lady who keeps the place."

CHAPTER IX

OFF ON A RUSH

THE boys liked their boarding place very much, and were soon made to feel at home. Mr. Hadley left them, promising to call after supper, and, while the meal was being waited for, Blake sent his uncle a letter telling of their safe arrival. Poor Joe felt rather lonesome at having no one to whom to write, for he was alone in the world, as far as he knew. But he did not entertain his gloomy thoughts long, for there was so much that was new, strange and interesting in prospect.

"I wonder what our first work will be?" he said to Blake, just before the supper bell rang.

"Learning some of the rudiments of the game, I fancy," replied Blake. "I don't even know enough to turn the handle of the moving picture camera."

"Neither do I, but I guess Mr. Hadley will tell us."

The photographer came over after supper, arriving about the time the boys' trunks did. He

71

found the lads sitting in the parlor, looking rather embarrassed, for they knew no one at the place; and, though they were not altogether unused to social life, they were typical country boys in a sense, not used to pushing themselves forward.

"How would you like to come and see some moving pictures, boys?" Mr. Hadley asked them. "I don't suppose you had much chance up there in Fayetteburg, and if you see some I may be able to explain certain things, as we go along, that will help you in the work."

"That's just fine!" exclaimed Blake, and a little later they were in one of the many moving picture theatres that dot New York's busy streets.

"Look!" suddenly exclaimed Joe, as a new reel of film took the place of the one that had about run out as they entered. "There's C. C. Piper!"

"By Jove, so it is!" agreed Blake. The two boys were talking in whispers until Mr. Hadley said:

"You don't need to keep so quiet, lads. The actors in this drama don't speak, and you can't interrupt them. As long as you don't talk too loud when the music is playing, you won't be obliged to whisper."

"He's as natural as life," commented Joe, as

they saw their new friend doing some comical scenes.

"Yes, that's C. C., all right," put in Mr. Hadley. "Old Gloomy Gus is right on the job. That's one of his best stunts. I made the film for him some weeks ago. It was a hit, too."

"Doesn't it seem strange to make pictures and then drop in some place and watch them being thrown on the screen?" asked Blake.

"Oh, I've gotten used to it by this time," was the answer. "I like to drop in the different places, and listen to the comments of the crowd. That's the best way to tell whether a film is a success or not. Often I get valuable hints that way. I'll be anxious to see how our new idea is received, and I may have you boys go about nights, listening to criticisms of our moving picture news sheet."

"That will be easy work," declared Joe. "Fancy being paid for going to a moving picture show!"

"It's all in the game," declared the photographer. "But watch this film. To see C. C. now, you'd never imagine he was so gloomy; would you?"

"No, indeed," the boys agreed, and they joined in the laughter that greeted the antics of the comedian.

"Just how are moving pictures made, anyhow, Mr. Hadley?" asked Blake, during a short intermission in the performance, when the reels were being changed.

"Well, it's rather hard to tell you in a few words," replied the photographer, "but I'll do the best I can. Later I'll give you something of the history of the business.

"In the first place, you know, you have to have something in motion to photograph, and this can be anything from a horse race to a volcano in action.

"In fact, the first moving pictures, if you could call them that, were of a horse galloping. Well, say, you have your scene selected. The next thing is a camera. The moving picture camera is in a way like all other cameras, in that it provides for the focusing of the image or picture on a celuloid film, made very sensitive to light. Only in a moving picture camera there is a long, narrow ribbon of film, that passes behind the lens, being moved in a series of jerks by mechanism worked by a handle. A shutter opens and closes, and every time it opens it makes a picture on the little square of film that, for a fraction of a second, halts behind the lens. Thus an exposure is made, and when you have a lot of them on a continuous reel of film, you have the beginning of a moving picture."

"And I suppose," said Blake, "that when you develop the pictures and dry them, they're all ready to be shown on the screen?"

"No, indeed!" exclaimed the photographer. "There is a lot of work yet. So far you only have what is called a negative picture. That would not do to show, for the blacks are all white, and the whites are all black. What is needed is a positive film, now, just the reverse of a negative, and this is secured by printing. Otherwise we would have to take hundreds of reels of the same scene, for one reel is needed for each projecting machine. But with one negative, any number of positives can be made, and it is these positives that are sent to the various theatres.

"How do they make positives?" asked Joe.

"Well, briefly explained, in this way: The negative film, with its contrasts of black and white, is laid on another strip of film of the same size. This second film is slightly different from the other in thickness and in sensitiveness to light. The two films are placed in a suitable machine that is light-tight, and then a brilliant light is placed in front of the lens. The films are now moved forward, together, in short jerks, and exposures are made just as when the original pictures were taken. Then the positive is developed when it has all been exposed. It is dried, and then it is ready for the projecting machines, and can be shown in various places. From one negative, or master reel, a number of positives can be made."

"Oh, that's how it is, eh?" remarked Blake. "I always wondered how they got so many reels of the one picture. I see now."

"But how is it thrown on the screen?" asked Joe.

"Oh, in somewhat the same way as magic lantern pictures are shown," explained Mr. Hadley. "The positive reel is passed in front of a brilliant electric light, and focused through a lens on a white screen. About sixteen pictures are shown every second, and they go so fast, one being whisked out of our vision before the image of the other has quite faded from our brain, that we think we actually see the pictures move as in real life."

"But they do move," insisted Joe.

"Yes, they do, in a way, but if it were not for what is called the 'visual persistence' of the human eye, moving pictures would not be as delusive as they are."

"'Visual persistence,'" murmured Blake.

"Yes. In plain language, that means that the

brain and eye persist in seeing an image after it is really no longer visible. Just as when you have looked at, say, a red spot on the wall for a long time—a stationary spot—when you close your eyes you still seem to see it."

"I've noticed that," remarked Blake.

"That's just the way it is in moving pictures," went on the photographer. "A man may be shown turning the knob of a door in one picture. A sixteenth of a second later the next picture is thrown on the screen, and it shows the door open a crack. Then it seems to open wider and wider, each successive picture showing an advance. But the brain, being somewhat sluggish, holds each view for the fractional part of a second after it has been whisked off the screen, and in this way, instead of the man opening the door by jerks, he appears to do it naturally, by continuous motion."

"Say, but that's interesting!" exclaimed Blake. "How did they find out how to do all this?"

"Oh, that would take too long to explain. Here comes a good picture. It's one made by our concern, of our road company, though I did not take it," and the beginning of a Western drama was thrown on the screen.

The boys enjoyed the little show very much, and their heads were rather in a whirl when they got back to their boarding house that night. They were early at the moving picture studio next morning, but Mr. Hadley had not yet arrived.

"Just amuse yourself until he comes down," suggested C. C. Piper, who was studying a new part. "I'm afraid it's going to rain," he added, looking out at the cloudless sky and sighing.

The boys wanted to laugh, but did not. C. C. was certainly a queer character, they thought. They were watching the start of a little playlet when Mr. Hadley suddenly rushed in.

"Come on, boys!" he cried. "Right on the job! I've got something good this time for our moving picture paper. Grab up those things, and trot along!" and he indicated several boxes, while he caught up an automatic camera and pressed a tripod into Joe's hands.

"What is it?" cried C. C. Piper.

"An elevated train has partly gone off a high trestle. I'm going to picture it!" cried Mr. Hadley. "Come on, boys!"

CHAPTER X

THE AUTOIST

"How did it happen?" asked Blake, as they sped down the hallway toward an elevator.

"Where is it?" demanded Joe.

"How did you hear of it?" came from Blake, before either of their first two questions were answered.

"I had a tip on it from police headquarters, just as I was coming down to the office," was the answer. "It happened up at One Hundred and Tenth street—where the elevated is very high. It ought to make a dandy picture. I want to get there before the wrecking crew removes it, so I can show the men at work. Lively, boys!"

"Anybody hurt?" asked Bake.

"Some, I believe. One car fell and was smashed. The others hung on the rails."

"This is getting excitement with a vengeance!" exclaimed Joe, as they crowded into the elevator, for which Mr. Hadley had signaled.

"Shoot her down, Jim!" the photographer said

to the elevator lad. "I've got to get to One Hundred and Tenth street on the jump."

"Some jump, boss," remarked the colored lad, with a grin.

"I can do it in a taxi," declared the man. "Come along, boys!"

They had dropped from the top floor of the skyscraper at express speed, and both Joe and Blake felt a ringing in their ears and a sinking sensation at the pit of their stomachs, due to the quick descent, and the difference in air pressure from the top of the elevator shaft and the bottom of the pit.

"Hi, there!" called Mr. Hadley to the chauffeur of a taxicab, which was standing at the curb. "Get us to One Hundred and Tenth street in a hurry—elevated accident."

"In you go!" exclaimed the man. His motor was already whirring, and hardly had Joe and Blake tumbled into the machine with the moving picture camera and spare reels of film, than there was a grinding of gears and they were off.

"I hope we get there in time to see it," murmured the photographer. "If I can get some good views we can finish a few positives by tonight, and, with the fire of yesterday and anything that may turn up this afternoon, I can show some lively scenes right hot off the bat."

"I suppose," said Blake, "that a moving picture newspaper will have to serve up fresh happenings just as a printed journal does?"

"That's right," agreed Mr. Hadley, "and it's a good deal harder to do, too, in a way. We haven't quite got moving picture production down to the fine point they have in printing a newspaper. We're handicapped, but we'll make good yet.

"Now you boys just stick close to me, and do what I tell you. I'll want you to hand me things, and maybe work the handle some. All you've got to do is to turn slowly and evenly. It sounds easy, but it isn't. Some persons think it's about like grinding an organ.

"But, as a matter of fact, you have to keep a uniform speed; and this is hard, as there is always an inclination to slow down. For instance, I knew one operator who was learning. He'd taken some fast scenes, fire engines, auto races and all that, and one day he was sent out to get a big parade scene—I forget what it was about. Well, as it happened, the marching was rather slow, and the operator unconsciously slackened his speed in turning the handle, to sort of correspond with the slow procession. The result was his film was spoiled, but he was a corker on fast subjects.

"You must always remember to turn the crank at the same speed whether you're photographing a bullet in flight or a lame dog walking along a fence. Sixteen pictures per second is what we want, and, no matter whether a moving object is slow or fast, the same rule holds good."

"But I should think," said Blake, "that if they took the pictures too slowly they could throw them on the screen faster and so make up for it."

"It may seem curious, but it can't be done," said the photographer. "The mistake can't be corrected."

"Then I guess we'd better not try to take any pictures until we learn more about it," suggested Joe.

"Oh, you can soon pick it up," went on Mr. Hadley. "You can't learn any younger. Of course, it takes some experience to know just how to focus for the picture, and what kind of film to use for certain subjects, as well as the size of the stop, or diaphram opening, which governs the amount of light that enters the camera. But you'll get all that in time."

He leaned forward and rapped on the glass of the taxi window.

"Can't you hit it up a little more?" he asked the chauffeur.

"I'm afraid to," the man called back over his shoulder. "There's a motorcycle cop been following me for half a dozen blocks now, and only that I've a pull with him we'd be pinched now. If I go faster he sure will get us."

"All right, then," agreed Mr. Hadley. "We don't want to lose time going to a police station to give bail. But make all the speed you can."

The chauffeur nodded, and after several quick glances behind, he opened up a trifle more.

"He's dropped back," he explained, to those in the taxi. "The cop, I mean. I guess it's safe to take a chance."

The auto dashed ahead, the two boys looking out on either side as they passed through the busy streets. It was a new experience for them.

"If we ever hit anything," said Joe, in a low voice, "good night!"

"Forget that kind of talk," suggested Blake, with a laugh. "You're as bad as C. C."

"That's right," assented Mr. Hadley. "Don't be looking for trouble. This isn't very fast. We'll soon be there, though. Guess I'll see if everything is in readiness."

He began testing the mechanism of his camera, so as to make sure it worked right, and that there would be no delay. This was no easy task in the rocking, swaying cab, but Mr. Hadley was like some newspaper reporters—used to doing things under difficulties.

Once, as they reeled along, they narrowly

missed collision with an auto coming out of a side street. There were yells and excited shouts, and a policeman held up a warning hand, but the chauffeur did not appear to see him, and went on.

Again, turning a corner, they skidded dangerously, and for a moment were on two wheels. Joe and Blake looked rather apprehensively at one another, but Mr. Hadley scarcely glanced up from what he was doing.

"We're some moving picture ourselves," declared Blake, in a low voice.

"That's what!" agreed his chum.

And behind them there came a sudden clanging of a gong, rapidly rung.

"What's that, the police patrol?" asked Joe, who had heard one the night before.

"Ambulance," briefly replied the chauffeur, for the front window was open and he could talk to the occupants of his machine.

"Ambulance, eh?" exclaimed Mr. Hadley. "Then we must be getting near the place. Get ready, boys."

By this time they were nearing the scene of the accident. Excited crowds could be seen rushing toward the place, and the chauffeur had to slow down to avoid accidents. A little later he swung up to the curb and stopped.

"This is as far as I can go," he said. "They have stretched police lines."

"All right—that's near enough," declared the photographer. "Wait here for us. I'll want to go back in a hurry if I get any pictures. I'll be showing them to-night."

"Look! Look!" cried Joe, suddenly. He pointed upward, and there, above their heads, clinging to the elevated structure, was a car, hanging so far over that it seemed it must topple into the street any moment.

"Fine!" cried Mr. Hadley, but he meant it from a moving picture standpoint, and not to rejoice in the accident.

"There's something else!" cried Blake, pointing to where the crowd was thickest. A moment later the concourse parted, and they could see where a car lay, smashed into fragments. It had fallen from the high structure to the street.

"Some are hurt, too," cried Joe. "They're carrying them out."

Several ambulance doctors, in their white suits, were caring for the injured, of whom there were a number. As our friends moved away from the place where the taxi had stopped another of the clanging hospital vehicles dashed up.

"I've got to get this!" cried Mr. Hadley. "Be

ready, boys. Here you!" he called to the driver of a heavy truck. "Are you in a hurry?"

"Not much, boss, or I wouldn't be standing here. I've got a little time. Why?"

"Because I want to hire you. I want to put my moving picture machine on your truck, so I can focus it above the heads of the crowd. Is it a go, for a five-spot?"

"It sure is. Hop aboard!"

"Come on, boys!" called the photographer, and a little later, with the aid of Joe and Blake, he was adjusting his camera on the tripod. The box containing the unexposed film was set in place, the one to receive the reel after it had been shown was likewise fastened, the handle adjusted and, after the camera had been focused, it was all ready to take pictures.

"Get me up as close as you can," directed Mr. Hadley, looking about for a vantage point. He wanted the sun at his back.

"Can't go through the police line, boss," said the truckman.

"Yes, we can," was the quiet answer. "I've got a permit, just like a newspaper reporter. I saw to that. Drive on."

A policeman tried to stop them, but on being shown the official pass, waved his hand, lowered the rope, and the truck, with the moving picture machine on it, went close to the wreck.

"A bad smash!" exclaimed Mr. Hadley, as he focused his machine. "Now, boys, when I begin to turn you hold the camera steady, for this isn't going to be easy to take. And stand by to do whatever else I need."

The work of the rescue was under way. Fortunately, the car that had left the rails did not contain many passengers, but all of them were more or less hurt, for the vehicle was split open by the fall.

Getting his focus, Mr. Hadley proceeded to turn the crank, and the moving pictures were being made. The boys looked on curiously, not a little proud that they had been let through the police lines, which held so many back. There was really little for them to do yet, but they were gaining experience.

There were sorrowful scenes being enacted, scenes of haste and of efficient work on the part of the doctors, and the moving picture machine recorded them all faithfully. Then along came the wrecking crew, and by pointing his camera upward, the photographer got some views showing the overhanging car being pulled out of danger. Then the ambulances were shown dashing off to various hospitals.

"Get ready with that extra reel of film," commanded Mr. Hadley, when he had secured some excellent views. "I'll need it in a minute."

Blake stooped to pick it from the bottom of the truck, while Joe was helping to steady the camera. As Blake turned, his eyes saw, on the inner fringe of the crowd, a man seated in a powerful racing car. Something about the machine itself, as well as about the driver, caught the lad's attention and held it for a moment.

"Here you go with that film!" called the photographer. "Hand it over. Why, what's the matter, Blake?" for the lad was staring at the autoist.

"Look!" exclaimed Blake. "There's the man who ran down Mrs. Randolph!" and the boy pointed directly at the individual.

CHAPTER XI

"You're right!" came from Mr. Hadley, after a moment's inspection of the man in the auto. "That's the chap, sure enough. I'd know his face anywhere after I made those enlarged photographs. I wonder if we can——"

But at that moment there came a cry from the crowd, and a scramble among those who pressed as close as they could to the smashed car.

"Something doing!" yelled Joe, who was steadying the camera. Blake had not taken his eyes off the man, and the lad managed to pass the photographer the extra roll of film.

"One of the ambulance horses trying to run away!" said Mr. Hadley, taking his attention off the autoist long enough to see what was going on. "I'll snap it!"

The restive horse required considerable attention, frightened as it was by the strange sights and sounds, and there was considerable danger to the injured and spectators at the scene of the accident.

Realizing that this would make a good section of his film for the moving picture newspaper. Mr. Hadley was industriously grinding away at the handle of the machine.

"They've got him under control," Joe finally announced. "But, Blake, is that man there yet?"

"Yes, and he hasn't seen us so far. He's in with a lot of other autos and he's going to have his own troubles getting out. I wish we could—"

He did not finish, but Joe knew what his chum was going to say, and so, too, did the photographer. He looked at the lads with a slight smile, and remarked:

"You're thinking of that reward, I guess?"

"That's right," admitted Blake. "I've got a warrant for that man, and if I could get near enough to ask a policeman to serve it——"

"There's no reason why you can't or shouldn't," went on Mr. Hadley. "I can manage this machine for a few minutes now, and if you want to slip away, and see what success you have, why, try it. If you don't come back soon, I'll know that you've caused his arrest, and you want to look out that he doesn't get away."

"He's looking over here now," said Joe, in a low tone. "I think he sees us."

"Quick—duck down!" exclaimed Blake. "Get behind the camera!"

"But he'll see Mr. Hadley," objected Joe, "and he'll probably recognize him."

"I don't think so," was Blake's opinion. "He didn't have a very good view of him in the first place, at the time of the accident, and he can't see anything but his back now. Come on, Joe; we'll take a chance at that two hundred dollars."

The two lads made their way to the end of the truck, which was still in position within the police lines. There was less excitement at the scene of the accident now, but Mr. Hadley was still taking moving pictures of the various activities, for he knew that a New York crowd is probably the most curious in the world, and in spite of the metropolitan character of the population, even the slightest incident serves to attract a throng. It was on this feature of human nature that Mr. Hadley relied for interest in his moving picture "newspaper."

"Take care of yourselves, boys!" he called. "If the police question you, just show 'em this pass. It's mine, but I won't need it as long as I stay here. And look out for accidents," he added. "I don't just like the way those fellows are hauling back that overhanging car," he went on. "A little more and it will slip down to the street just as the first one did. I guess I'll get ready to take some snaps of that."

Ascertaining by a look in the direction of the autoist that he was still there, Joe and Blake made their way through the throng of policemen, reporters, ambulance drivers and surgeons, and others who were helping in the work of caring for the injured.

"There's a policeman right by him," said Joe, in a low voice. "We can show our warrant to him and ask him to make the arrest."

"That's right," agreed Blake. "And, say, I've just thought of what I'm going to do with my share of the reward, if we get it."

"What?"

"I'm going to buy a moving picture camera, and go into the business."

"Fine! So will I, and maybe we can start a moving picture newspaper of our own."

"That would be great; but first, let's see if we can get the reward."

The boys made their way through the press of people, and were gradually nearing the object of their quest. Once or twice they were stopped by officers, but a display of the paper Mr. Hadley had given them was sufficient to insure them immunity from being put out from the police lines.

"There he is!" exclaimed Joe, a little later, when they came to a comparatively clear place, and had a view of the autoist. "He hasn't seen us, but watch the way he's staring at Mr. Hadley. I'm sure he suspects something, and if he sees that we are gone he may imagine he's due for trouble. What do you say?"

"That's about what I think. Come on. Make a dash for it. I guess we can. Oh, there he goes, Joe. He's seen us and he's going to get away in his car!"

At the same moment Joe noticed that the autoist was looking in their direction. A look of recognition shot over his face, to be replaced by one of annoyance, if not of fear. The boys saw him lean forward and touch the switch of the self-starter on the dash of his machine.

Instantly the throb of a powerful motor told that the ponderous auto was ready to start. The man gave a look back of him, and saw that he was practically hemmed in. Yet he did not hesitate.

"It's the same one, all right!" cried Joe. "I can see where the mudguard was broken, and has been fixed. It's him, all right!"

"Yes, and he's going to get away, I'm afraid," said Blake.

The ponderous car was slowly moving backward, as the autoist threw in his reverse gear and released the clutch pedal. At once a storm of protest arose from two cars in back of his, for they were in danger of collision.

"Here, where are you going?" cried one of the owners.

"Getting out of here!" snapped the man.

"But you'll crush my radiator. Hold on, there! You can't get out of here!"

"I'm going to, I tell you!" cried the man the boys were after.

"He doesn't care anything for the rights of others," murmured Blake. "Just like when he ran down Mrs. Randolph. I hope we can catch him."

"It doesn't look so," said Joe. "Hold on, there!" he yelled, motioning to some policemen who had come up to see the cause of the dispute. "Don't let that man get away! He's wanted on a warrant."

Joe pointed to the autoist, who was still keeping his car going backward. The policeman turned to look, but at that moment the man in the machine directly behind the big racer was obliged to reverse his gear to prevent his lamps and radiator from being damaged.

"You're a fine fellow!" he shouted angrily at the reckless autoist. "What did you crowd in here for, if you want to get away in such a hurry?"

"That's my affair!" snapped the other.

"Well, I'll make it mine!" declared the man who had been obliged to get out of the way.

"Don't let him escape!" cried Joe, but it was too late. The careless autoist had backed far enough to give himself an opening. Before any of the police could get near him, even had they understood what was wanted, the man, with a quick shifting of his gears, threw them into place, turned on more power, and with a thunder of the exhaust shot away from the crowd.

"There he goes!" cried Joe.

"And our reward," added Blake, bitterly. "We were just too late."

"But we'll have another chance at him," declared his chum. "It was something to even see him in New York, and now that we know he is in this vicinity, we'll be more than ever on the lookout. But we'd better be getting back to Mr. Hadley. He may need us."

"I fancy we'll have to do some explaining to the police," spoke Blake. "Some of them are headed this way. Well, we can say——"

But Blake never completed that sentence. At that instant there echoed a crash overhead, and a shout of warning came from many throats.

Without realizing it, the two boys had gotten under the high elevated railroad structure, near the place where the car overhung the street. Looking up, they now saw this tottering, and the wrecking crew frantically trying to prevent another crash, though the vehicle was, of course, emptied of occupants.

"Look out!" yelled Joe. "She's going to fall!"

"Yes, and Mr. Hadley on the truck will be hit, too!" cried his chum. "Scoot for it, Joe!"

They sprang to one side—an example followed by all in the danger zone, and they were not a moment too soon, for an instant later the car, tearing loose from the hoisting chains, fell into the street with a terrific crash, and a cloud of dust hid Mr. Hadley and the truck from sight.

CHAPTER XII

STARTING THE PICTURES

"THAT must have fallen on him!" gasped Joe, when he could make his voice heard above the echoes of the crash.

"He was almost under it, that's a fact," agreed Blake, though because of the dust that had arisen they could not see plainly. With one accord they started for the place where the second car had fallen. A policeman stopped them.

"You can't go there!" he cried.

"We've got a pass," said Blake, displaying it. "We're with the moving picture outfit."

"Oh, all right, then. I did see you on the truck. Well, go on, but look out for yourselves. I'm afraid you won't find much of the outfit left."

With heavy hearts Joe and Blake made their way around the heap of debris, into which the railroad workmen were now frantically digging to see if any persons were pinned underneath. Then the wind blew aside the cloud of dust, and Blake cried:

"Look! He isn't hurt at all!"

Joe glanced to where he had last seen the truck containing Mr. Hadley and the moving picture outfit. It was intact, and the intrepid operator was industriously grinding away at the crank, taking picture after picture of the newest scene in the accident.

"That's right—he doesn't seem to be even scratched," murmured Joe. "But it was a close shave, all right."

"It sure was," agreed Blake. "He must have been within a few feet of the car when it fell. Lucky the truck horses didn't run away. And he's taking pictures as if nothing happened."

"He has nerve!" complimented Blake. "Talk about the perils of war, they're not much ahead of this moving picture business, as far as I can see."

"Sure," murmured Joe. "Now let's see if we can help him. He may need us."

"Well, boys, how'd you make out?" asked Mr. Hadley, calmly, as they climbed up on the truck again. The driver had by this time unhitched his horses, because, as the boys learned later, they were so restive that they moved the wagon, thus endangering the success of the pictures.

"No luck at all," explained Blake. "He got away."

"Did you get hurt?" asked Joe of their friend.

"Not a bit. I was right on the spot, though. Couldn't have been in a better place to get some snaps. I was afraid that car was going to fall, and I got ready for it."

He continued to grind away at the crank, occasionally swinging the camera about, or tilting it upward on the base to get different views.

All about was confusion, for, while no one was injured by the fall of the second car, there was much excitement, and the rescue of those injured when the first vehicle crashed down was interrupted.

But now order was coming out of chaos, and soon the last of the afflicted ones had been taken away. More men from the railroad came and began the work of clearing away the debris.

"I guess I've got about all the pictures I need," said Mr. Hadley, a little later. "The worst is over, and the rest of the views would be ordinary ones. Besides, we don't want to give the public too much of one thing. We must vary our moving picture newspaper. Come along, boys; we'll pack up and get back to develop these."

The two lads, little used to such scenes of excitement as they had just passed through, were glad enough to get away, though they were fast losing their country characteristics and becoming genuine New Yorkers.

Mr. Hadley paid the truckman, and, making their way to the waiting taxicab, the boys and their employer were soon at the theatrical studio.

There Joe and Blake were permitted to witness the making of a moving picture film. In the dark room the exposed reel was removed from the camera box and wound on a sort of frame to go into the developing tank. In due time the thousands of tiny pictures. each one inch by three-fourths of an inch in size, began to show up on the narrow ribbon of film.

When properly developed the pictures were "fixed" in a chemical bath to prevent them from disappearing when exposed to the light. Then, when the negative film was dried, it was ready to be used in printing the positives.

Of course, all this took some time, and while waiting for the various processes to be completed, Mr. Hadley took the boys about the factory, explaining various details to them.

"You see we get the film, ready for exposure, from the manufacturer," he said. "There are several places where it is made, and in one factory there is made every week more than seven million feet of film.

"Then before it can be used the film has to be

perforated on each edge so that the sprocket teeth in both the camera and the projecting apparatus can pass it rapidly and evenly behind the lens. These perforations, or holes, are made to what is known as the Edison standard; that is, sixty-four perforations per foot, and each hole is about one-eighth of an inch in width, and about half that in height. But they have to be absolutely true, or the pictures would be spoiled. There are several machines for making these perforations."

"Say, there's a lot to this moving picture business; isn't there?" remarked Joe.

"There certainly is," agreed Blake. "We're just beginning to understand it."

"Oh, you've got plenty to learn," said Mr. Hadley, with a smile.

By this time the printing of the positives was under way, and this, when it was finished, would mark the next to the last stage of getting out the moving picture newspaper. The last would be the showing of the pictures themselves.

"I think we'll be able to show our picture in several theatres to-night," said Mr. Hadley, at the close of the day's work. "I have attached some lengths of other films, showing street scenes, to the ones I took of the fire and the elevated accident. If you boys would like to see them——"

"Would we!" exclaimed Joe and Blake in the same breath.

"Then I'll stop for you to-night and we'll take in the same theatre we took in before," finished the photographer.

That night the two lads eagerly awaited the showing to them of their first view of a moving picture newspaper. Of course many of my readers have seen them, if not American versions, then the French variety of topical happenings. Very interesting they are, too, I think you will agree, and it is no wonder that Joe and Blake were anxious.

The first scenes shown were those of an Indian drama, and while the boys liked this very much, they wished it would end. But not until another reel had been disposed of, showing some peculiar tricks, was there flashed on the screen the announcement:

HADLEY'S MOVING
PICTURE NEWSPAPER.

"Your paper!" gasped Blake. "Why, I thought it was part of the Film Theatrical Agency's business."

"This is a little surprise to you," said the photographer. "I have arranged with Mr. Ringold to take over the newspaper part of the business myself, providing I can make it go. That is why I wanted lads of my own choosing to help me. If all goes well I will give up the making of drama and story films indoors, and do nothing but outside work. There is a big field for it."

"There's the fire scene!" suddenly exclaimed Joe, as there flashed into view the depiction of the conflagration Mr. Hadley had taken the day the boys arrived. It was very interesting, but they were more anxious for the elevated accident to show. Soon that came.

"There it is!" exclaimed Blake, as the scenes they had witnessed that day were now thrown in bold relief on the white screen.

"Why—why—it's as real as can be!" cried Joe.

"Listen to what the people are saying around you," said the photographer, in a low voice.

CHAPTER XIII

SUCCESS

For a moment or two Joe and Blake did not quite understand what Mr. Hadley meant. Then it came to them. He had said he wanted to know whether his plan of supplying daily to the public pictures of the happenings in New York and vicinity would be a success. Now was the chance to find out.

In the half-darkened theatre the murmur of voices could be heard on all sides. At first there were only murmurs of approval—for the pictures, from a mere photographer's standpoint, were excellent. But soon the character of the views themselves began to make an impression on the audience.

"By Jove! That's great!" exclaimed a man back of Joe.

"It sure is," agreed another, who sat near Blake. "Why, I saw that very accident myself this morning."

"You did?"

"Yes, and now I come here and see it thrown

on a screen. I used to think it was wonderful when I could, perhaps, witness something—say a baseball game or accident—and on my way home meet a newsboy with the papers containing most of the details of the happening. That was great, but this goes it one better. I can actually see over again in picture form what I saw only a few hours ago in reality. I wonder how they do it?"

"I don't know," answered his friend. "It's all a mystery to me."

"And it was to us, a few days ago," whispered Blake to Joe. "But we've got the inside track on them now."

"That's right," agreed his chum.

"Oh, see!" exclaimed a childish voice, just in front of the boys. "There's the train Aunt Mary rode in, but she didn't get hurt."

"No, darling," said the little one's mother. "Aunt Mary wasn't in that train. She missed it, and took the one after it, or she might have been hurt."

"I'm glad she missed it," went on the little girl. "I don't want Aunt Mary hurt. But them people is hurt, I guess."

"Yes, dear; and see, that horsie is trying to run away."

"That's the ambulance horse," said Joe. "Remember that time, Blake?"

"I sure do. It's just as if we were seeing it over again, isn't it?"

All around were exclamations of wonder at the faithful depiction of the scenes. There was no doubt that Mr. Hadley had "made good."

"It's a success, all right," murmured Joe.

"It sure is," declared his chum.

"Yes, I guess we're safe in going ahead," decided Mr. Hadley. "Now I must get busy and perfect my details. It is going to be quite a problem to work out, but I guess we can do it."

They remained until the last of the Hadley pictures were shown, and then, as the next film was one they had viewed before, they came out of the theatre. Few, if any, of the audience realized that the quiet-appearing man, accompanied by two bright-looking boys, had been responsible for their seeing the depiction of the elevated accident.

"Yes, it's a success," murmured the photographer, as he saw the throng outside the place, waiting to get in. On boards in front of the moving picture theatre were notices of the attractions within, and the "newspaper" was featured. It seemed to attract much attention.

"Well, there's only one thing I'm sorry for," said Joe, as he and Blake went to their boarding place that night.

"What's that?"

"That that autoist got away."

"Oh, yes, that was a sort of disappointment, but it wasn't our fault. Anyhow, we've proved one thing."

"What's that?"

"If he's been in New York once, he'll be here again, very likely; and we may get a chance to spot him sooner or later."

"That's right. And if we do he won't get away so easily. I want that reward."

"So do I. You didn't notice his license number, did you, Joe?"

"No; it was so covered with oil and dust that the figures didn't show. I believe he did that on purpose—put oil on the plate so the dust would stick fast and cover up the number. Lots of 'em do it."

"I know it. Well, we'll keep on the lookout. If we go around much, taking moving pictures, we'll have lots of chances to hunt for him. I guess we'd better write and tell Mrs. Randolph that we had a clue, but it got away. Then she'll know we haven't given up." His chum agreed with him, and the letter was prepared.

In return they got word that Mrs. Randolph was as anxious as ever to catch the reckless autoist, and had increased the reward to five hundred dollars for his arrest.

"Five hundred dollars!" murmured Blake.

"Two hundred and fifty apiece!" cried Joe. "Say, we must get it!"

"We'll do our best," answered his chum.

Mr. Hadley received many congratulations when he got to the office the next morning, for word of the success of his moving picture newspaper had preceded him. The films had been shown in several New York theatres that night, as well as in some near-by large cities.

"But it won't last!" predicted C. C. Piper, who seemed in an unusually gloomy mood, as he got into a clown's dress to rehearse some odd pantomime scenes for a fairy play that was to be depicted. "The public will soon tire of it, and you'll have to come back to making ordinary plays."

"Oh, cheer up, Gloomy!" exclaimed Mr. Hadley, who seemed to be always looking on the bright side of affairs. "You must have gotten out of the wrong side of bed this morning; or weren't your eggs done to suit you?"

"That's all right—laugh and be gay!" murmured the comedian, "but it'll be a failure, you see if it won't."

"And then you'll say, 'I told you so,' I suppose," replied Mr. Hadley, with a laugh. "Well, you'll not get the chance."

"What makes you so positive?" asked the

gloomy funny chap, as he dabbed some streaks
and spots on his face to give himself a more grotesque appearance.

"Did you ever see the public get tired of reading the newspapers?" asked the photographer.
"I guess not. Of course, some papers fail, because there are too many of 'em. But people
still want their evening or morning journal every
day, no matter whether they had one the night
before or not.

"They want to see what's happened, and this
principle of curiosity is what I depend on to make
this thing a big success. The public will always
want to know what Hadley's paper is going to
picture for them next; and I'm going to give 'em
the best that I can. Why, C. C., if ever you have
anything happen to you, I'll be there—or Joe or
Blake will—and make moving pictures of it."

"Then I'll take good care that nothing happens," said the comedian; "though I have a sort
of feeling that I'll be in an accident before night.
I hope it isn't an elevated one, anyhow."

"You haven't predicted rain yet, Gloomy,"
Miss Shay reminded him.

"Haven't I? Well, it's going to turn out un-
pleasant before night, I'm sure. But, here we go
again. Come on, little one!" and catching up
Birdie Lee, who was to take part in the play with

him, C. C. whirled her about in a dance, in strange contrast to his gloomy mood.

"I guess you can't change C. C.," mused Mr. Hadley. "Has Mr. Ringold come down yet?" he asked of one of the men on the studio stage.

"Yes, a few minutes ago."

"Then I'll see him, boys, and arrange about our new business. I want to get quarters for ourselves where we can be undisturbed, and yet get out on the jump when anything big happens. And I want telephone service, and other things."

"Will we have to leave here?" asked Joe.

"Well, perhaps we'll take offices somewhere else in the same building. I'll have to be near the developing and printing plant, you see. Now I'll go in, have a talk with Mr. Ringold and see what he says."

CHAPTER XIV

THEIR FIRST ASSIGNMENT

"Say, this is all right; isn't it?"

"All to the honeycomb, I should say!"

"Some different from the little attic room I used to have at Mr. Bradley's farm house."

"Yes, and it's a heap sight better than hoeing corn or potatoes, or even getting in hay."

Joe Duncan and Blake Stewart, the moving picture boys, were thus talking as they sat in the new quarters of Mr. Hadley's illustrated "paper." Two weeks had passed since they were with him at the scene of the elevated wreck, and in this time they had learned much of the business; though they still had much yet to grasp before they would become experts.

The conference with Mr. Ringold had been satisfactory, and he had arranged with Mr. Hadley to let him use part of the big building for offices; while the developing and printing plants were at the service of the photographer to get his pictures ready for the theatres. Of course,

Mr. Ringold shared in the profits.   Joe and Blake were paid fair salaries, with the promise of a raise as they became more expert.

They were employed in Mr. Hadley's office, and were his personal assistants.   There were other helpers in the place, and occasionally Mr. Hadley was called on to photograph scenes in the theatrical studio, when there was a rush on. But in the main he was now making nothing but moving pictures of events of popular and daily interest.

Telephones had been installed, so that news of accidents or other events of calmer interest could be sent in, and Mr. Hadley, or his assistant photographer, would rush off to get the views.

As yet Joe and Blake had not been allowed to take any pictures on their own responsibility, though they occasionally turned the crank of the machine at which Mr. Hadley was presiding, when he was busy with some part of the mechanism that needed adjusting.

"I want you boys to learn the rudiments of the business, and all the tricks and crankiness of these machines, so you will know what to do in emergencies," said their chief.   "Anybody can learn to grind the crank if he keeps at it long enough, but everybody can't understand the ins and outs of the apparatus in one lesson, or even two.   So, while it may seem tedious to you, it's for your good."

The boys realized this, and, as they sat there looking about their new quarters, and contrasting them with those on the farms they had so recently left, they were wondering when would come their chance to go out and make moving pictures all by themselves.

"I wonder what will be our first stunt?" mused Blake.

"Oh, probably taking some street scene, where nothing particular happens," answered Joe. "That's the easiest to do, and if we happen to spoil it there's no great harm done, as there would be if we went after some big fire or accident and didn't get results."

"That's right," agreed his chum. "You can always go back and get some view of the same street scene, whenever you want; for the street stays there, and the people are about the same from day to day. But you can't get a fire to repeat itself, or an accident, either. And yet I would like to try my hand at a big stunt, Joe."

"So would I. Oh, well, our time will come. But, say, we haven't had much luck finding that mean autoist."

"No, he seems to have disappeared. That was a nice letter Mrs. Randolph wrote us. She said she was glad we had not forgotten, and that she was just as angry as ever at him, and determined to sue as soon as he was arrested."

"That's right. He looks able to pay damages, judging from the kind of a car he rides around in."

"Yes. It's got some speed, too. He may be arrested for going too fast, some day; and then we could get hold of him."

"Not much chance, as long as we don't know his name nor the number of his car. However, we'll keep on the lookout whenever we have a chance. But we've got plenty of work to do. Have you sent out all those circulars telling about the new films that will be ready this week?"

"Yes, and I guess——"

He was interrupted by the ringing of the telephone bell.

"I'll answer," said Joe, as he was nearest to it. The person at the other end of the wire proved to be some one who wanted to inquire about getting some of the newspaper films for his theatre, and as the boys were now well up on the business end of Mr. Hadley's affairs, they were able to make the satisfactory arrangements.

"Got anything exciting on?" came the inquiry.

"There's a tugboat collision in the Hudson. Happened this morning. You can have a film in time for to-night's performance," answered Joe.

"Good! Got anything else?"

"Collapse of a new building in the Bronx. The view shows it after it's fallen, when they're carrying out some of the workmen and trying to raise the girders with derricks."

"Good again! I mean, of course, I'm sorry any one was hurt, but we want some excitement. Send up the films as soon as they are ready."

Joe promised, and a little later Mr. Hadley came in, having been out to get the pictures of an East Side riot, when the children in one of the schools were compelled to be vaccinated, and their mothers objected, thinking the children were in danger.

"Got some good films," announced the photographer, as he sent them up to be developed and printed. "Anything doing?"

The boys gave details of the business that had come in.

"Everything seems to be going satisfactorily," went on the photographer. "I think I'll let you boys try your hands now. Take one of the old cameras and go over to Chinatown. Get scenes of anything you think would be interesting. Remember what I told you about focusing; get the sun at your back every time you can, and don't be afraid to push your way in.

"Lots of times a crowd is so curious that they shove around you and spoil things. Tell them to get in front of the camera, and you'll take their pictures. This always fetches 'em, and gets 'em away so you have room to work. Go out and try your luck, boys."

Joe and Blake were a little fearful that they might make a failure, for they had never gone out by themselves; but they realized that the only way to learn was by doing things, so they got ready.

Proceeding to Pell street, one of the centres of New York's Chinatown, they found a good place for their camera, and began snapping the queer and shifting street population. At first they attracted no attention, but finally a crowd gathered, and persisted in getting so close that the resultant pictures would be too large to make satisfactory views. By dint of much explaining, using some of the methods suggested by Mr. Hadley, the boys succeeded in getting the Chinese, and their street neighbors, to move back.

In the midst of taking the scenes a "slumming" party arrived. This was a big "rubberneck" auto, as they are called—a sort of automobile 'bus, carrying many passengers. They make regular trips through Chinatown, and the conductors explain, or pretend to, the various scenes, many of which have been connected with crime.

"That will make a good view," said Blake, who had relieved Joe at the handle.

"Yes, we're having pretty good luck," assented his chum. "Say, look at that fellow trying to climb up on the auto."

One of the roughs of the street, thinking he saw a good chance for fun, persisted in an endeavor to board the big vehicle. He did manage to get up on top, and then proceeded to annoy some of the ladies of the party.

The conductor remonstrated, but the companions of the rough urged him on, and finally the conductor resorted to physical argument. This was just what the rough wanted, and for a minute there was quite a fight, while the women of the party screamed and clung to their male escorts.

The conductor was getting the worst of it when the chauffeur of the auto decided to take a hand. He attacked the rough from the rear, and then it was "all over but the shouting," as Joe said. The rough was soon disposed of and retired, much discomfited, while the "slumming" party went on.

"Say, we got every bit of that!" exclaimed Joe in delight. "I think that will be some film."

"I think so myself," agreed his chum, and so it proved.

On being developed and printed, the pictures of the street scene and the fight in Chinatown turned out to be remarkably clear, and well centred and focused. Of course the boys had very good luck, which did not always follow them, as you shall see. But their first assignment was satisfactorily covered, and they were complimented by their employer.

"You will soon be going out on bigger stunts," he told them, and they hoped the time would speedily come.

Meanwhile they were given more instruction in the groundwork of the business. They took apart and put together the complicated cameras and projecting machines, so as to know how to repair them if damaged. The speed of different films was studied, and then came some lessons in photography, the values of light and shade, the proper stop or diaphragm to use, and how to get good results under adverse conditions.

"It isn't as easy to make pictures in some countries as it is here," said Mr. Hadley. "In the tropics it is particularly difficult to keep the film in good condition, because of the heat and moisture.

And in very cold countries, sometimes, the movement of the film in the cameras generates electric sparks, that make queer light streaks across the pictures."

The photographer told some incidents connected with taking pictures in Africa and other jungle countries.

"Say, wouldn't it be great to go and get pictures of wild beasts?" exclaimed Joe.

"Or volcanoes and earthquakes!" added his chum.

"You boys don't want much," said Mr. Hadley, grimly. "But you may come to it. When I started in I had no idea I'd wind up like this."

The moving picture newspaper continued to grow and prosper in the next few weeks. The boys were getting more and more insight into the business, and liking it better as they progressed.

They had yet to "pull off a big stunt," as Blake expressed it; though they were hoping every day that Mr. Hadley would let them try their hand at a big accident. Their chance came when they least expected it.

One afternoon both Mr. Hadley and his chief assistant photographer were out. The former had gone to Jersey City to get views of a tall chimney that had served its usefulness, and was to be blown down; and the other was at a big street parade.

Suddenly, the telephone in the office rang. Blake jumped to it, and Joe heard this half conversation:

"What's that—a big fire? In a tenement house? Yes! Making rescues, eh? Of course we want to cover it. Much obliged. We'll be right there!"

He hung up the receiver with a bang, and cried:

"Joe, our chance has come!"

CHAPTER XV

THE TENEMENT FIRE

JOE DUNCAN gazed at his chum for a moment. He did not seem to comprehend. Then he began:

"Why—what——"

An instant later he understood.

"I have it!" he cried. "We'll go, and——"

"Take moving pictures of that tenement fire!" finished Blake. "It's our first big chance to show what we can do, and I know we'll make good."

"But maybe Mr. Hadley——"

"We can't get at him to ask him whether he wants us to or not. It's a big fire, the police operator says. It was fine of him to tip us off. It's a big fire, and the theatres will certainly want pictures of it."

"All right! I'm with you. But Mr. Hadley has both our new cameras with him."

"That's nothing. There's the old one here. That will do to take up in the fourth or fifth story of some building near the one that's burning. Then we can borrow one of the big theatrical machines. They have a lot of 'em ready for emergencies, all loaded up."

"Good! I'll go borrow one."

"And I'll get things ready down here. Oh, if we can only make good!"

Something of the excitement of the fire seemed to communicate itself to the boys. Yet, in all their haste, they worked with a certain method. They had not watched Mr. Hadley go out in a rush on big affairs not to know what to do.

While Joe was being shot upstairs in the elevator to borrow a moving picture machine from the parent company of the moving picture newspaper concern, Blake was getting the old camera ready, with its reels of film. This machine was of a small type, but still a good one, and was more easily carried than the larger ones.

"How are we going to get there?" asked Joe, as he came back with the borrowed apparatus.

"Taxi—of course!" exclaimed Blake. "We don't want to lose any time. Just scribble a note and leave it on Mr. Hadley's desk, telling him where we've gone. He may get back soon, and want to come up to superintend operations."

"Oh, I hope he lets us get these pictures all alone," said Joe.

"So do I," responded his chum; "but still, we want to make sure that we do get them. It's like a reporter on a newspaper going out on an assignment—he doesn't want to fall down on it."

"All right—I'm with you!" exclaimed Joe, as he finished writing the note. "Come on!"

A little later they had jumped into a waiting taxicab, and were being whirled toward the burning tenement. While yet some distance off, they were made aware of the size and importance of the blaze. The sky had become obscured by drifting clouds of smoke, and there was a smell of burning wood.

A little nearer, and the boys could hear the puffing of the engines, the shrieks of the whistles as they called for more coal, and the clanging of bells as the reserve wagons dashed up.

"It's a big one, all right!" cried Blake, the excitement getting more and more into his blood.

"Fourth alarm," said the taxi chauffeur shortly. "A lot of people hurt, I'm afraid."

"I hope there aren't any harrowing scenes," murmured Joe. "One thing I don't like about this business is that we have to show so much of the sad side of life."

"Well, it's there—every one knows it, and we're like a newspaper—obliged to give all the news we can get," replied his chum. "Look out!" he cried, suddenly.

The taxi driver had been about to dash across

a side street, when a big red auto, belonging to one of the deputy chiefs, whirled out, narrowly escaping collision with the vehicle in which rode the boys.

"Close shave—that!" exclaimed Joe.

"We get used to 'em—in New York," replied the chauffeur. "I've been in a lot of collisions in my time, and I'm alive yet."

He drove on a little further, until a policeman, seeing him, held up his hand.

"Nobody allowed past here," called the officer. "Go around the other street."

"How about it, boys?" asked the taxi man, for he knew them, having taken them and Mr. Hadley to several accidents.

"We've got passes," answered Blake, for their employer had taken care to get them police permits, such as the regular newspaper reporters have, admitting them within the fire lines.

"All right—nothing more to say," replied the officer, when he had glanced at the cards. "Go as far as you like, but don't go too close. There have been one or two explosions."

"Explosions!" cried Joe.

"Yes; there were clothing-cleaning and pressing places in the basement of this tenement, and the gasoline, or naphtha, they had stored has blown up. Some one said that started the fire, but

I don't know. I've just arrived. Reserves from four precincts are here."

The taxi now swung around a corner whence a good view of the blazing building could be had. Hitherto the boys had only seen a black cloud of smoke, fringed with yellow tongues of flame.

"Some fire!" cried Joe, as he got ready to alight from the cab with the camera.

"Right!" exclaimed Blake, grimly. "Now, if you'll stay down here, and get what you can, I'll try and get in some building and go up a few flights to make views."

Losing no time, Joe found himself a place of vantage, where he would have a good view of the conflagration; and Blake left to seek a place higher up.

The tenement was a large one, many stories high, and occupying an entire block. The whole interior seemed to be ablaze, though at either end there was a portion from the windows of which no smoke, as yet, poured out.

But the great black masses were pouring straight up from the roof, flames spouting at times, showing that the top covering had been burned through, making a perfect chimney draught for the fire.

"Some blaze!" gasped Blake, as he shoved himself through the crowd and entered a hallway that he saw would lead him to the middle of another tenement across the street. The occupants of that were beginning to move out their household goods, and Blake knew he would not be stopped if he entered one of the apartments, and took pictures by thrusting the camera out of a window.

He guessed right, and he was not stopped on his upward journey. Selecting an apartment about in the middle of this tenement, he made his way to the front window. The place seemed deserted.

As the moving picture lad looked out on the conflagration across the street, he saw firemen swarming up the front of the building by means of scaling ladders. These are long poles, with cross bars at frequent intervals, and a long, toothed hook on the end. The hooks are caught in window sills, and by successive mountings a fireman can thus reach the roof when other means fail.

"Getting ready for the rescue work!" exclaimed Blake, as he prepared his camera for action. "We'll get some dandy films if we have luck."

He looked down in the street and saw where Joe had established himself on a hook and ladder truck. The vehicle was stationary, the horses and most of the apparatus having been removed from it. It made a fine vantage place for the moving picture machine.

"Joe's on the job!" murmured his chum, as he saw the handle of the larger machine turning. "Now I've got to get busy."

From below, Blake heard many sounds. The puffing and coughing of the engines, the hiss of steam, jangling of bells as autos, auto engines, chiefs' and officers' vehicles dashed to and fro; the clang of the trolley repair wagon, that sought to get the hose either up over the tracks on "shears," or by building a temporary track over the lines, with openings for the water conduits to pass through. The blocking of traffic is always a serious matter.

Hoarse commands were shouted through big trumpets or megaphones. Firemen were swarming up the face of the building on scaling and extension ladders. Some carried hose, and others were evidently prepared for rescue work, with hatchets in their belts, ropes over their shoulders and smoke helmets on their heads.

Ambulances could be seen and heard, and in one place Blake saw a number of firemen making ready the circular life net.

"Some one is going to jump!" thought the lad. "I wish the smoke wasn't so thick. I'm afraid I can't get any pictures."

An instant later a brilliant beam of light shot through the murkiness. At first Blake thought it might be the flash of an explosion; but an instant later he saw that it was one of the portable searchlights.

"Good!" cried the lad. "This will make it light enough." Usually the big lanterns were only used at night, but in this case the smoke was so thick that artificial illumination was needed.

Blake focused his camera, being sure now that he would get some fine views. The light was just right, and as he looked on the ground glass screen he could make out the moving figures of the firemen swarming up the face of the building. As they climbed they were caught and pictured on the sensitive film.

Suddenly there was a shout, and Blake, looking, saw a figure leap from the roof. It was a man, and he had evidently been trapped there.

"He'll be killed!" thought the lad; but, looking down, he saw the life net spread out and the firemen waiting. Hastily he swung the lens of his camera downward, catching the body in its fall, and he also got a view as it struck the net, bounced up and was safely caught by several of the "smoke-eaters."

Then a fireman appeared coming down a scaling ladder, and carrying a woman over his shoulder.

"I've got to get that," said Blake, aloud, and once more the film registered the rescue.

There was a period of comparative calm, as sometimes happens at a big fire. The smoke seemed to drift away, and Blake worked the handle industriously. Then, suddenly, he was aware of a great shouting below him. The crowd seemed to be pointing at the building he was in. Leaning out of the window he looked to right and left, temporarily stopping the machine.

He saw a pall of smoke shooting from a casement not far from where he was working. It was followed by a tongue of flame.

"This building's on fire!" thought Blake, with a chill of fear clutching at his heart. "Some sparks must have blown in an open window and started a blaze. I wonder if I'd better get out?"

He thought a minute, and then, as he saw more firemen performing rescue feats, he decided:

"I'm going to stick! I've got to get these pictures. I'll stay here until it gets too hot for me!"

CHAPTER XVI

THE DIVER

Swirls of smoke flew up into Blake's face. A shift of the wind had brought them, and also a hot whiff of flame.

"It's beginning to burn fierce!" exclaimed the lad, but he did not cease grinding the crank of the moving picture machine. For a moment smoke obscured the view of the burning tenement across the street, and Blake was afraid he would get no more pictures; but then the fierce white beams of the searchlight cut through again, and he knew that the stirring scenes were being registered on the film.

"I wonder how Joe is making out?" mused Blake. He leaned far over and looked down, meanwhile ceasing to turn the handle. He could see his chum, now and then, when the smoke was blown aside, industriously grinding away.

"Joe's on the job," murmured Blake, and then, as several of the other unfortunates, trapped on the roof, leaped into the life net below, the moving

130

picture boy trained his camera on them to catch them in downward flight, as well as when they landed in the meshes.

A little later several firemen again appeared on the face of the structure, carrying down unconscious forms, and this made just the material Blake wanted; though his heart ached for the unfortunates who, if they were not hurt, had lost their little all in the fearful blaze.

A shout below caused him to look down. He saw several new pieces of fire apparatus arriving, and then, at the bottom of the building, whence he was taking pictures, he saw ladders beginning to be raised. A deputy chief, in his white rubber coat and hat, was signaling to some of the smoke-eaters.

"I guess they're going to turn some water in here," said Blake aloud. "Well, they'll need it soon, for it's getting hotter."

More frequently now the swirls of smoke from the windows on either side of him blew into his own casement, and again came that stifling breath of hot air.

"How much longer can I stand it?" thought Blake. He looked at the register on the side of his camera and saw that he still had a number of feet of film to expose. It was the last reel, for he had changed twice.

"I'll finish up!" he thought, grimly. "Might as well get all I can."

But even as he registered this determination, he staggered back, so fierce was the wave of heat.

Immediately afterward, though, he saw a cloud of sparks arise from the top of the burning building across the street, followed by a dull concussion.

"Part of the roof has fallen in!" exclaimed Blake. "I'm going to try and get the scene when it all goes. It will be a dandy—from our point of view; though probably the owners and the fire insurance companies won't like it."

Once more he trained his camera on the structure that was now a mass of flames. No need now for the rays of the searchlight. There was more flame than smoke, and the scene was brilliant. Blake took another look down the street. He could not see Joe now, and he realized that his chum must have been forced to go back, as indeed had many of the firemen, for the tenement was in danger of collapse at any moment. In fact, some of the fire apparatus was being withdrawn.

So interested was Blake in what was going on that he did not see what was taking place about the structure where he was. In a way he had become aware that the building was becoming more and more filled with smoke; and he heard, rather than saw, that several streams of water were being poured in the windows adjacent to him. It never occurred to him that he might be in great danger.

Suddenly a helmeted head was thrust up from below, directly in front of him and the camera.

"Get out of there!" cried the lad, instinctively. "Do you want to spoil my pictures?"

"Get out of here yourself, you chump!" cried the fireman. "Do you want to lose your life? This place is going. It's a tinder-box—we can't save it, I'm afraid."

Half unconsciously Blake continued to turn the crank, until a peculiar clicking told him that the last of the reel of film had passed behind the lens. He could get no more pictures, so there was no use in remaining longer.

"All right—thanks!" he called to the fireman. "I'll come down."

He made his camera secure, slipped the exposed reels of film in their light-tight boxes onto clips on the back of his machine, and tossed the carrying strap over his shoulder. He had not used a tripod for this small machine.

As Blake turned away from the window he heard the fireman shout something, but what it was he could not distinguish. At the time he took it for a warning to hasten. But a moment later he knew that it was not.

For, as he reached the stairway by which he had ascended, he was driven back by a puff of smoke, through which he could see the angry, licking tongues of flame.

"Trapped!" cried Blake. His heart faltered, but only for a moment. Then, realizing that to stay where he was, in that fierce heat, would melt and spoil his precious exposed films, he turned back. The fireman, who had climbed up a scaling ladder, had leaped into the room Blake had just quitted.

"Hey! What's the matter with you?" growled the "smoke-eater." "Are you crazy with the heat? I came up to get you. The chief seen you from below and thought you couldn't get down. I didn't know you were taking pictures."

"I was, but I'm through now," said Blake. "I'm ready to leave."

"All right—drop that box and I'll carry you down. You don't look heavy."

"Drop this box! I guess not much!" cried Blake, choking as a puff of smoke struck him in the face. The fireman winced, too. "I'm going to take this camera with me," declared the boy. "It contains some dandy views of this fire for our moving picture paper. I'm not going to leave it."

"But I can't carry you and that, too."

"You won't have to!" replied Blake. "I'll go down the ladder myself, and carry this. I can climb—I was brought up in the country."

"Good for you, lad! So was I. But let me take part of it. I can manage that." Blake realized that the weight might be too much for him, so, hastily taking off the extra boxes of reel, and explaining to the fireman the need of keeping them away from the heat, the lad prepared to descend.

"Go slow, and don't be afraid if the scaler sways a bit, lad," advised the fireman. "Don't look down, and you won't get dizzy. I'll go first, and if you fall I'll catch you."

"I won't fall!" declared Blake, with conviction, though he felt a nervous tremor at the prospect of descending five stories down the face of a burning building on so frail a support as the scaling ladder. There was no fire escape available at this point.

There was no help for it. He must save his life and the pictures—if he could. He began to realize some of the perils of taking scenes in a great city.

Out of the window he climbed, and down the scaling ladder after the fireman. Once he began, he grew less nervous, and he could hear the shouts of the crowd below. Blake wondered if Joe was watching.

Down and down he went, guarding the precious camera, with the last reel of film in it, as best he could. At times smoke would swirl out from the windows they passed, hiding the ground from them. Again the heat of flames could be felt.

Past floor after floor went Blake, a ladder on each story dangling from the window ledges by means of the big toothed hook.

"All right! You're on the last one!" cried the fireman, encouragingly. Blake started down it, scarcely able to see from his smoke-smarting eyes. He felt some one grasp him, and guide his feet to solid earth.

"Bully boy!" cried a voice in his ear, and he looked around to see Joe. "Here, give me the camera!" yelled his chum. "I guess you're about all in, aren't you?"

"Oh, not so much; did you get any pictures?"

"Yes, some fine ones, until I had to skip out."

"And you've got to skip out of here right now!" interrupted the fireman, yelling at them. "This place is soon going to be too hot to hold any of us. Get back before she topples over!"

The structures on both sides of the street were

now blazing fiercely, but, as the flames were yet some distance up from the ground, it was bearable in the centre of the highway. But the fire was working down.

"I guess we'll have to go," agreed Blake. "We haven't any more film, anyhow."

"No, but we can go back and get more!" cried Joe.

"That's right. Come on, then."

Leaving the burning structures behind them, for the firemen to fight over, the lads sought out their taxicab.

They were soon at the office, arriving just as did Mr. Hadley, who had hurried back on hearing of the big tenement fire. That he was delighted by the enterprise of his pupils goes without saying.

"I couldn't have done better myself!" he declared. "It was the best ever! Now you get washed up and take a rest, and then rush these films to be developed and printed. I'll go there and get some more scenes."

"Can't we go?" begged Blake.

"Say, lad, don't you know when you've had enough?" asked the photographer, with a twinkle in his eye. "You do as I say. Besides, I need some one to see that these films get out in time for use in the theatres to-night; and there won't be much more that I want at the fire, anyhow."

The boys realized the wisdom of his words, and soon they were superintending the making of the moving pictures from the exposed reels they had brought in.   While the first were being made Mr. Hadley came in with more, announcing that he had enough of the fire.

The pictures were a great success, and audiences crowded many theatres to witness them, further increasing the reputation of Mr. Hadley's moving picture newspaper.   And, in a way, Blake was a hero of the hour, for some of the newspapers devoted considerable space, in their fire story, to the lad who stuck at his post to get moving pictures until he had to be rescued by a fireman with scaling ladders.

"Whew!" exclaimed Joe, when he and his chum were ready to go to bed that night.   "Some day, Blake!"

"That's right.   A hot time all around.   But I liked it."

"So did I.   Wonder what we'll get next?"

"I don't know—maybe a Chinese wedding."

But it was no peaceful and ordinary scene that the moving picture boys were next called on to get.   Early the next morning, when they reported for work, Mr. Hadley, with a whimsical smile, greeted them with:

"Well, boys, I think I'll send you to sea to-day."

"To see what?" inquired Joe, not catching the meaning.

"To see the sea—in fact, to get pictures of a diver at work. You had so much of fire yesterday, that I think you'll be glad of a chance to take water."

"A diver at work," faltered Blake. "Will we have to go down——"

"Not to the bottom of the sea—no," interrupted the chief photographer. "There's been a small schooner sunk down in the lower bay, and a wrecking company is going to try to raise it. I have chartered a small tug for you boys, and, as I have an important engagement myself, I'm going to let you make these diving scenes. It won't be hard work—not that you're not capable of doing that if you have to—but about all we'll want is some views of the man getting ready to go down, some scenes of his disappearing below the water and when he comes up. Later we may snap the raising of the schooner if they raise it. Are you ready?"

"I—I guess so," answered Blake, wondering if he would get seasick.

CHAPTER XVII

THE BRIDGE JUMPER

"Well, boys, are you all ready for me?"

"Go ahead," answered Blake.

"And act naturally," advised Joe. "Don't think of us at all. We want these pictures to appear just as if some one was looking at you and you didn't know it."

"All right, boys. I'll do my best."

It was the deep-sea diver who had answered, and the moving picture boys had been giving him a few instructions, which he received in good spirit. The lads had come down the bay on the tug, and had reached a point near where the wrecking vessel was anchored, preparing to raise the sunken schooner. The latter's position under water was marked by a buoy.

Contrary to the fears of Joe and Blake, they had not been in the least seasick, for the water was calm, though there was enough motion to render the taking of pictures anything but an easy task.

Their tug had come as near as was practical
to the craft from which the diver would descend.
Aboard the wrecking tug was the apparatus; the
air pumps, the coils of hose, the life line, the
diver's suit, with its big copper helmet, the glass
eyes making it look like some grotesque fish, and
then the heavily weighted shoes, each one having
about thirty pounds of lead on the soles, to over-
come the buoyancy of the diver in his air-inflated
suit.

The boys, taking turns in working the cameras,
had made several yards of preliminary pictures,
and were now ready for the main ones of the
diver going down. The motion of their tug
somewhat bothered Joe and Blake, but they soon
got used to it.

"These pictures will have a swaying motion
when they're thrown on the screen," said Blake.

"Yes, maybe some of the audience will get seasick from looking at them," replied his chum; "as
I heard a theatrical crowd once did when watching a scene when the deck of a ship was shown,
heaving up and down and pitching and tossing."

"I'm going to put on the helmet now," called
the diver to the lads, from across the stretch of
intervening water.

"All right, go ahead," spoke Blake.

"Look pleasant, please," advised Joe, and the

diver smiled at them—a smile that was caught and imprisoned on the sensitive film.

The diver's assistants now placed the heavy copper helmet over his head, screwing it fast to the metal collar of his suit.   Immediately the air pump started working, the two men being at the cranks.   The air entered the helmet, was breathed by the diver, and then, after being expelled from his lungs, was forced out through an automatic and water-tight valve in the rear of the helmet. It is this expelled air that makes the string of bubbles which rise to the surface wherever a diver is at work.

The man, with a wave of his hands to the boys, looked to see that his life line and air hose were clear, and then stepped over the side to a ladder that led below the surface.   He had to move slowly on account of the weight of his shoes and diving suit, but the boys, mindful of the instructions of Mr. Hadley, turned the handles of the moving picture machine with the same speed used when making the views at the exciting fire.   I have already explained the necessity for this.

"There he goes!" exclaimed Joe, as the head of the diver disappeared below the surface.   "No use taking any more views until he comes up again."

"That's right," agreed his chum. "We can rest up a bit. He'll be down there an hour."

They got their machines in readiness to record the reappearance of the diver above the surface. He was only to do preliminary work at present, noting the lay of the foundered ship, and devising the best means of putting chains under her to raise her.

"This isn't going to take much film," remarked Blake, as he looked at the register on the side of the camera, and noted that only a few yards had been exposed.

"No, but it will be interesting," declared his chum. "Mr. Hadley wants to get as many different subjects as possible, and if we only get a few feet, as long as it's sensational, the theatre crowds will appreciate it. At the same time, a long film, like a big fire, goes well, too, I heard him say."

"That's right. Well, there's one thing about being out here that's different from being on land."

"What—the wetness?"

"No, but we don't have to be on the lookout for that mean autoist."

"He would hardly come out here, unless he had a hydroplane," agreed Joe. "I wonder if we'll ever land him?"

"Hard telling.   Well, we're all ready for Mr. Diver when he comes up."

The man appeared a little later, ascending sooner than it was thought at first he would.   But the moving picture boys were ready for him, and soon the camera was clicking away, showing the man arising, dripping wet, from the bottom of the bay, like some new kind of a mermaid.   The scene made a good one, for the day was bright, and the water offered a good contrasting background.   The diver's helmet was unscrewed and once more he could breathe as do ordinary human beings.

The boys had now completed their work, and, ascertaining that there would be no likelihood of raising the schooner that day, they started back for New York.

"I wish we could get something unexpected to use up the rest of this film," remarked Blake, as they neared the big city.

"So do I," agreed his chum.   "It seems a shame to stop work so early," for it was only about noon.

The tug which Mr. Hadley had hired for them was proceeding up the East River, for it docked on that side.   As the craft was approaching the Brooklyn Bridge, Blake, who had gone to the bow, uttered an exclamation of surprise, and pointed up to the great structure—wonderful even though others like it have been made.

"Look!" cried Blake to Joe. "Something is going on up there."

"That's right," came from his chum. "Look at the crowd!"

"There's been an accident!" declared the tug-boat captain. "Maybe a car-smash or somebody run down. There's too much traffic on that bridge, anyhow."

"An accident!" gasped Blake. "Oh, if we could only get it! We'd have a fine finish for our diving film!"

"Can't you snap it from here?" asked the captain.

"It's a little too far off to show details," replied Joe. "We might take a chance at it, though. What do you say, Blake?"

"I say let's do it. Look at the crowd! It's getting bigger every minute. Get out the camera, and we'll make a try."

It did not take long to focus the moving picture machine on the structure above them. But when Joe looked through the lens he uttered a disappointed sigh.

"The distance is too great," he said. "Can you put us ashore, captain?"

"I could, but it will take some time; and when you got there the best of it might be over."

"Then we'll try it from here," went on Joe, when he was interrupted by a cry from Blake.

"It's all right, Joe! It's all right. This will make a dandy picture from just where we are. Don't you see what it's going to be?"

"No—what?"

"A bridge jumper. There's a fellow getting ready to spring off that railing. Oh, if we can only snap him!"

"We've got to!" yelled Joe, changing the focus of the machine.

"There he goes!" cried Blake.

At that instant the figure of a man shot downward from the bridge structure, and the moving picture machine began clicking.

CHAPTER XVIII

RIVALS

"HAVE you got him, Joe?" asked Blake.

"Yes. We couldn't have a better place. He's coming down right in front of us. I wonder if it's a suicide, or if he's doing it on a wager?"

"For money, most likely!" exclaimed the tug captain. "There's easier ways of committing suicide, if one is bent on it. And a jump from the bridge is comparatively safe, if you hit the water just right."

"He looks as if he was going to," declared Blake.

"Where's the boat that's going to pick him up?" asked Joe. "I understood they always had one in readiness."

"There she comes!" exclaimed Blake. "A little motor boat, from the looks of it," he added, as a small craft shot out from behind a larger one, and made for the spot where the jumper would likely land.

"And here comes another," cried Joe, never

pausing in his work of turning the handle. "And, look—it's got a moving picture machine on board!"

Blake and the captain of the tug looked. They saw, coming toward them, a craft similar to their own, and in the bow, on a tripod, was a moving picture camera, with several men grouped back of it. One, whose arm movement betrayed him, was working the crank.

All this while, of course, the body of the bridge jumper was shooting downward, and Joe, by lowering the lens of his camera, kept it in focus. He wanted to show the minute the man struck the water.

Suddenly, from the other tug, came a hail:

"Hey, you fellows, chase out of that! This is our stunt!"

"Your stunt!" replied Blake, for he did not want Joe to take his attention off the jumper.

"Yes, we arranged for this. You fellows can't take any pictures of it. We paid for that jumper."

"But we *are* taking pictures of it, just the same," responded Blake. "And we're getting results, too."

"Get away from there!"

"Don't let 'em get those views!"

"We want 'em exclusive!"

"Run 'em down if they don't leave!"

These and other expressions were shouted at the moving picture boys as they continued to make views of the bridge jumper. Of course, all this had taken place in a few seconds, for though the Brooklyn Bridge is high, a falling body does not take long to get from it to the surface of the water.

Joe realized this, and he was directing all his skill to making a good series of pictures. The other tug, in the meanwhile, was coming nearer, as was also the rescue boat. But the advice of one of the hot-headed rivals to our heroes was not heeded. There was no ramming done, probably for the reason that to do so would have spoiled the chances of those who had arranged the jump to take views.

"There he goes!" cried Blake, as the man struck the water, feet first, with a great splash. "Did you get him, Joe?"

"I sure did, Blake. Now to snap him when he comes up."

"He'll probably swim toward the rescue boat," was Blake's opinion. "Point her over to the left a trifle."

His chum obeyed, and the rival tug, coming closer, the operator aboard her focused his machine on the same place, showing that Blake had guessed right.

"Get away from here!" came angrily from the rivals.

"Not much!" retorted Blake, stoutly. "This river is free to all!"

"But we arranged this stunt—you had no right to butt in on us," said one of the other men.

"We didn't mean to," said Blake; "but as long as we saw the man jump, and got some of the views, we're going to get the rest. I think——"

"There he comes!" suddenly cried the other moving picture operator. "Get out of my view!"

This last to some of his own friends who had, in their excitement, got in front of the camera.

The bridge jumper shot up from the water and struck out toward the small power boat that was waiting to pick him up. The rescue was soon effected, for the man was a strong swimmer, and, the boys learned later, a professional diver, who had taken this desperate leap at the behest of some moving picture men for a substantial sum.

As he was hauled into the boat and the craft moved off, Joe got the last of the views he needed, and stopped his machine. The other operator, having a little better position than had our heroes, had also gotten the series of pictures he wanted.

"I'll have the law on you for this!" he cried

to Blake and Joe. "You can't get away with our ideas that way! We'll fix you!"

"I guess we've got as good a right to photo scenes on the Brooklyn Bridge as you have!" snapped Joe. "Go ahead and sue us if you want to. We're from Hadley's Moving Picture Newspaper."

"Oh, I know where you're from, all right," growled the other man. Then his craft shot toward shore, following the rescue launch.

"Do you suppose he's going to try for more views?" asked Blake. "What else can happen?"

"No; the police will probably arrest that fellow," said the tugboat captain. "They always do when a fellow jumps off the bridge—charge him with trying suicide, and those fellows may want to get him in some scenes."

"Well, I guess what we have will do," spoke Blake. "We must get ashore now, and have these developed."

Mr. Hadley was delighted with the success of his young assistants, not only in regard to the diver, but the bridge jumper as well.

"These, with some I took to-day, will make a dandy illustrated paper for the theatres to-night," said the photographer. "But it's a surprise to me that we have rivals on our track. And yet I might have expected it. Everything in this business is copied sooner or later, and there's no way of getting a patent on some of the scenes. You didn't learn who those fellows were, did you?"

The boys had not, but later, when the diver was arrested, just as the captain had said, it developed that the pictures had been arranged for by a syndicate of men who were not only in opposition to the Film Theatrical Company, but also to Mr. Hadley himself.

"Well, if it's competition they're looking for, they'll get it," declared the photographer. "Two can play at that game, though I won't go out of my way to get the stunts they arrange for. We'll arrange some of our own, and beat 'em at their own game. I must get busy on this. Rivals, eh? Well, we'll be ready for them.

"Of course, you boys did just right to snap this jumper. You didn't know he was in the pay of the others, and we want all the odd scenes you can get. But after this we'll have some of our own."

The diving scene, which was shown in many theatres that evening, created a sensation, as did the bridge jumper, and the hopes of the rivals of our heroes to have an exclusive feature were doomed to disappointment.

The next few days were devoted on the part of the boys to taking various scenes about the city.

Some were gay and some pathetic, while not a few represented accidents and ordinary street happenings that would interest the public. Occasionally the boys failed to get good views, from various reasons, but in the main they did well.

In all their going about Joe and Blake kept watch for a certain powerful racing car and its occupant, for the thought of the reward was never long absent from their minds. But they had no success.

Meanwhile the rival moving picture newspaper men were busy, and often Joe and Blake saw them at the same scenes where they themselves were making views.

"I think I'll pull off a stunt to-morrow that will surprise them," said Mr. Hadley one evening. "You boys get here early, and we'll see what we can do."

CHAPTER XIX

A TRICK FILM

"WHAT do you imagine he is going to try?" asked Joe of Blake, as the two chums arrived at the office the next morning.

"I haven't the least idea. I've been reading up something of how trick films are made, in a moving picture book, and there are any number that might be worked. But most of them are indoor scenes, and our picture paper goes in mostly for those taken out of doors."

"How do they do the indoor ones?" asked Joe; "say one where a man smokes a pipe and a fairy jumps out of it?"

"It's easy when you know how," replied his chum.

"Well, maybe it is—but how?"

"First, the moving picture of a man smoking a pipe is made, just as if we made it ourselves. Then the camera is stopped.

"Then, on a second stage a big property pipe is placed, a pipe large enough for a real person

154

to get inside it, and the photograph is made of that, but at such a distance that the pipe seems to be the size of the one the man is using. Out jumps the fairy, and her picture is recorded on the film past the point where the man was snapped. When the film is reeled off before the audience there is nothing to show where the stop took place, and where the camera was focused on the real pipe of natural size to the large or property one out of which the fairy jumped, and it looks as if the sprite came out of the real pipe."

"I see!" exclaimed Joe. "I must get that book and read up on this."

"Of course, there were other scenes that took place with the man, the fairy, pipes, cigars and so on," explained Blake; "but all the tricks were worked on the same principle."

"I wonder if that's what Mr. Hadley is going to try?"

"I think not. He'll go in for out of door subjects, I think."

The boys did not have much longer to speculate, for Mr. Hadley soon arrived.

"Well, we're all ready for our trick picture," he said, briskly. "I've got it all worked out. But we'll need the help of our friend, C. C. Piper."

"Oh, it's going to be a funny scene," spoke Joe.

"Not necessarily, but I think Gloomy will fill

the bill. I'll go get him, and you boys can pre-
pare a couple of cameras. We may need them
both."

"Well, what's up now?" asked C. C., as he
came down with Mr. Hadley, and greeted the
boys. "You don't expect me to go out and do
stunts to-day, do you?"

"Why not?" asked the photographer, in some
surprise.

"Because it's going to rain, I'm sure; and I
had a twinge of rheumatism last night. I got it,
I guess, the day I did that rescue stunt out where
we picked up these boys."

"Oh, you get out, C. C.!" exclaimed Mr. Hadley. "What you think is rheumatism is indiges-
tion from eating too much, and not working
enough. And as for rain—why, there never was
a better day."

"Oh, it'll do something before night, I'm sure,"
went on the gloomy comedian. "But go ahead.
I might as well die first as last. What do you
want me to do?"

"Just take a little walk along certain streets and
out in the country with the boys," said Mr. Hadley.

"Ha! A walk in the country!" exclaimed C. C.
"We'll be starved, I know, for there won't be anything to eat, and I'll get all lame so I can't dance,

and there'll be bugs and stickers and—ugh! I don't see why I ever stay in this business, anyhow!" and C. C. sat down and began running over a new funny song he was learning.

"Oh, you're the limit, Gloomy!" declared the photographer. "I'd think you were serious if I didn't know you. But come on, now, I'll tell you what I want," and he proceeded to give his instructions.

With the two boys to make the pictures and work the cameras, C. C. left the studio building. They proceeded to a certain street, where, in accordance with their instructions, the comedian proceeded to walk leisurely along, stopping when he came in front of a certain tall building.

"I don't see where any trick picture is coming from on this film," objected Mr. Piper. "It's just an ordinary scene."

"It does seem so," agreed Joe.

"Better wait," advised Blake. "This is only the beginning. I don't know all the details, but I'm sure Mr. Hadley knows what he's about."

"Well, what's next?" asked C. C. "Shall I try to walk to the moon?"

"No, we're next to go out to Bronx Park," explained Blake; "and take pictures of you walking toward the beaver pond. When you get to the edge of it you're to stop."

"Oh, I'm to stop, eh?" asked C. C. "You're sure I'm not to keep right on and wade through it and get a lovely chill? Sure about that?"

"No, you don't have to do that." declared Joe, with a laugh. "Just to the edge of the pond. Then we'll walk around to the other side and you'll walk away from the shore."

"I don't see any sense in it," objected the comedian; "but I suppose I'll have to do it."

As they were about to go to the subway that would take them to the zoological gardens, Blake uttered a cry.

"Look over there!" he called to Joe.

"Our rivals!" gasped the other lad. "They've been spying on us!"

"Yes, and taking the same kind of pictures we have, of C. C. walking along the street," went on Blake. "They're just packing up their camera."

They all looked across the street, and there saw some of the men who had been on the tug at the time of the bridge jumping, and who had so strenuously objected to our heroes' presence.

"Hum! I must be in great demand, if a rival concern tries to snap me," murmured C. C. "I think I'll ask for a raise in salary."

"I don't imagine they got much—just you walking along the street, and stopping in front of the building," commented Blake, with a chuckle. "I wonder if they'll follow us farther?"

Whether the rivals did or not, the lads could not learn just then, for the other men disappeared around a corner as our friends went to the subway station.

"They must have had a spy watching our studio," explained Blake, as they were whirled along; "and they trailed after us. But I imagine they are up a stump, wondering what sort of a stunt we are trying."

"I'm wondering myself," said C. C. "You're sure I don't have to wade through that beaver pond? Because I might as well tell you now, as later, that I won't do it. I'm done with tank dramas."

"You won't have to," declared Joe, who, with Blake, had been instructed what to do on the outdoor end of the view.

The boys had almost finished taking views of C. C. walking toward the beaver pond, when a clicking off to one side attracted their attention, and they looked behind a screen of bushes to observe their rivals again trying to make the same sort of pictures as they were themselves.

"On our trail again," murmured Blake. "Well, it won't do 'em much good."

"Where next?" asked C. C., as he and the boys

got ready to leave. The rivals departed as soon as they saw that they were observed.

They did not address our friends, and Joe and Blake felt it would be better policy not to get into a discussion, for they knew that the rivals could not steal Mr. Hadley's idea—at least, not before the pictures were exhibited.

Other pictures of Mr. Piper were taken, some in Central Park, showing him stopping abruptly at the foot of the obelisk, others at the base of a big chimney, some more in front of tall buildings, and one just on the edge of a big sewer excavation.

"Well, this gets me!" exclaimed the comedian, when the day's work was over. "I don't see any trick here."

"And I guess our rivals didn't, either," chuckled Blake; "for they gave up some time ago. But the next part of the picture will be made in the studio. Mr. Hadley is going to do that himself to-night, and then this will be ready to be shown to-morrow."

"I must see it!" declared Christopher Cutler Piper.

CHAPTER XX

THE BURNING SHIP

"Well, I guess we're all ready to proceed," announced Mr. Hadley that night, when he and the boys were gathered in one of the big rooms of the studio building—a room brilliant with electric lights.

"Where's Mr. Piper?" asked Joe, for he did not see the gloomy comedian present. "Don't we need him, if you're going to take some more pictures of his walk?"

"Not at all," answered Mr. Hadley, with a laugh. "In fact, this is Mr. C. C. Piper," and he produced a small, doll-like image of a man dressed exactly as Mr. Piper had been that afternoon. "This is Gloomy's understudy, I might explain," went on the photographer. "He will act his part in the trick film."

The boys were rather mystified, especially when they saw Mr. Hadley arrange to suspend a moving picture machine from the ceiling, so that the lens pointed toward the floor. On the floor was laid a strip of black cloth, and the figure of the doll, which it appeared could be wound up and made to walk in a most natural manner—this figure was placed at one end of the black cloth strip and some electric lights were focussed on it.

"Now, boys, you'll wonder at it, when you see how simple it is," said the photographer. "I am going to wind up this doll and have it walk along the black strip. As it is black, no impression will be made by it on the sensitive film, but the mani-kin, being dressed in light clothes, just as C. C. was, will be vividly taken against the black back-ground. Now we're ready."

He started the doll in motion, and the moving picture camera overhead, but off to one side, be-gan clicking. It was an automatic one, operated by a small electric motor within.

"The camera is taking pictures of the doll in mo-tion," said Mr. Hadley; "and the lens is adjusted to such a point that when the image is thrown on the screen it will appear exactly like a man. The doll, who is, you might say, C. C. Piper, is now walking up the front of the building where you took your first photos."

"But there is no building here!" objected Blake.

"Well, you took several feet of film of the building after C. C. had stepped out from in front of it, just as I told you; didn't you?" asked the photographer.

"Yes," replied Joe.

"Then it will be all right. I am going to use two films, as you can soon understand. The first scene will show Mr. C. C. walking along the street, just as he actually did. No trick about that, of course. He comes to the front of the building, and then calmly proceeds to walk up the front of it, just as if he was a fly."

"Why, how can he?" asked Blake.

"Because he only *seems* to do so," explained Mr. Hadley. "What the audience sees going up the front of the building is this doll image. I will take the film we are now making, put it on top of the one you took showing just the building, and will print the two films as one. By joining this one we are now taking to the one you took, at the point where Mr. C. C. disappears from the picture and the doll comes in, it will look as though the actor really kept on walking—right up the side of the building. When he reaches the top he gets on the roof and disappears from view, just as the doll does," and Mr. Hadley caught up the automatic manikin, and stopped the moving picture machine.

"This is our trick film," the photographer explained. "Now we'll show C. C. walking across the beaver pond in the Bronx Park. It will be done the same way—by having the doll, which resembles C. C. enough to deceive the audience, walk across the black strip. Then I'll superimpose that film on the one you took of the beaver pond with the real C. C. out of sight. In this way it will look as if C. C. walked up to and across the water. In the same way we can make it look as if he walked up the big chimney."

"And Cleopatra's Needle in Central Park?" asked Joe.

"Exactly. You took some views of the obelisk with C. C. out of the way, didn't you—after he stopped at the foot of it?"

"Yes," replied Blake.

"Then it will be all right. In the same way I'm going to make it appear that he walks on air over the big sewer trench, and does various other things seemingly impossible. See how easy it is?"

The boys were astonished, as indeed many persons are when they see trick moving pictures, and learn how simply they are produced. An auto riding around the rings of Saturn is brought about by a little toy auto skimming around a cardboard ring, held by invisible wires around a painted illuminated disk that represents the planet. And yet, with all this, some trick pictures, seemingly simple, are very difficult to bring about so as to appear natural. Many intricate devices are necessary, and long practice and rehearsal needed to produce perfect results. Then, too, the cutting off of the film at the right place, and the joining to it of another section, taken at another time, is no easy task.

I might add here that while this story of the moving picture boys is, in a way, a fanciful tale, told of imaginary characters, all of the incidents set down actually occurred in real life. I have merely taken other characters than the real ones. And every event here set down about the moving picture industry, trick film, newspaper scenes and so on, is actual fact, as can easily be proven. In future books I will go more into details, while still retaining the story feature.

"Well, this is certainly great!" exclaimed Blake when the taking of the trick films was accomplished.

"It sure is!" agreed his chum. "I want to see that on the screen."

"The Wonderful Walk," as the new film was called, was ready for exhibition the following night, and gave pleasure to thousands in many theatres, even while mystifying them. Our heroes witnessed the projection in one moving picture place, and laughed heartily at the comments made as C. C. hurried up the side of a building, up to the top of the chimney, and did other seemingly impossible feats.

All sorts of guesses were made as to how it was done, from saying the man was pulled up with invisible wires to that he used a balloon or an aeroplane which did not show. But Joe and Blake knew the secret.

This picture went so well that others, some more complicated, were made in the following days, and, though C. C. complained, as he always did, that something direful would happen, nothing did.

Several weeks passed, and the moving picture boys were getting to be experts. They were intrusted with important assignments and did their work well. But they had not succeeded in locating the reckless autoist, though they had several letters from Mrs. Randolph, making inquiries.

One afternoon, when Joe and Blake were alone in the place, Mr. Hadley and his principal assistant being in a distant city, the telephone rang, and Joe, who answered it, heard from the ship news reporter this message:

"There's a vessel afire down in the lower bay. Do you want to get some 'movies' of her?"

"Do we?" cried Joe, as he hung up the receiver, with a bang; "I guess we do. Come on, Blake! More trouble!"

"What is it?"

"Ship on fire down the bay. I'll get the big camera, and you can take that new hand automatic. We'll see how it works."

"I'm with you! Go ahead!" And they were soon rushing toward the Battery, where they knew they could hire a swift tug.

CHAPTER XXI

THE BALLOON ASCENSION

"THERE she is, Joe!"

"Yes, I see her. Afire all over, too, Blake."

"That's what she is. And look, there's the *New Yorker*, the big harbor fire department boat, steaming down there for all she's worth!"

"That's right. Say, we ought to get some dandy pictures this time!"

"I believe you. Can you get up any more speed?" asked Blake of the tug captain. The boys were standing near the pilot house of the craft they had hired in a rush to go to the burning steamer.

"More speed!" repeated the seaman. "I've got extra weights on the safety valve now. If you don't want me to blow you up, you'd better not ask for more speed."

"Well, we surely don't want that to happen," said Joe, with a smile; "for it would spoil the moving pictures we hope to take, and we couldn't even get views of ourselves in mid air."

"No, but some one else could," spoke Blake, in a low voice; "and I guess they'd like to see us out of business."

"Who's that?" inquired Joe, as he began making ready one of the cameras on the bow of the tug.

"Our rivals. That other concern that's trying to get up a weekly moving picture newspaper in competition with ours."

"Is that so? Where are they?"

"Coming up in the rear fast. They've got a better tug than we have."

Joe took an observation, and with a pair of marine glasses was able to identify, on the bow of the tug astern, the same men who had objected to the taking of the views of the bridge jumper.

"It's them, all right," said Joe to Blake. "They must get tips the same as we do, and follow 'em pretty closely, too. But we have just as good a chance as they have on this stunt, and they can't claim they originated this one."

"Hardly, unless they set the steamer afire themselves."

"They didn't do that," went on Joe. "The ship news reporter told me it was spontaneous combustion of some chemicals in her hold. The fire was discovered some days ago, according to the wireless reports, but they battened down the hatches and turned steam into the hold. But the fire got hotter and hotter, and finally broke out as they got into the lower bay. It certainly is going hard now."

"I should say yes. Better begin taking views, hadn't you?"

"I started some time ago."

"Good! Then I'll get to the stern and pick up what I can there, and we can make a combined reel. I want to show the fire boat in action if I can."

They were now rapidly approaching the burning steamer, which was enveloped in flame and smoke. Her officers, crew and the few passengers aboard were leaving by small boats, which were being lowered at the side where there were no flames or smoke for the time being. The steamer was a "tramp" vessel of no special line, though of good size.

Joe was busy taking many excellent views on his reel of film, the tugboat captain getting him in good positions, when the fire boat dashed up and began playing several streams of water from her powerful pumps on the seemingly doomed craft.

"Swing us around broadside," requested Joe. "Then Blake and I can both get views of the *New*

Yorker at work, so, in case one film is no good, the other will be."

"All right!" sung out the captain, and he swung his wheel over. By this time denser and blacker clouds of smoke rolled up from the burning ship, and the boys were in the midst of getting some of the best views they had ever taken, when they heard the sharp clang of engine room bells near them. Without pausing in the turning of the handles of their machines, they glanced around and saw the tug of their rivals.

"Can't you fellows drop astern a little and let us get in?" came the half growled request from the man in charge of the picture machine.

"We could, but we're not going to!" snapped Joe. "We were here first, and, while we didn't arrange this little exhibition, we're going to insist on our rights. You've got a good view where you are."

"Shove 'em out of the way!" said one of the men in a low tone, though not so guarded but what the captain hired by our heroes heard.

"No you don't!" he cried. "If you try any of those tricks, I'll make a complaint against you to the harbor master. We're going to stick here."

"Oh, go ahead and get the pictures—stop chinning," commanded one of the others in the party of the rivals.

Whether it was intended or not was never known, but it is certain that the other tug suddenly started full speed ahead. Her blunt nose rammed the other craft just at the point where Joe was standing at his machine. There was a shock, a cry of dismay and warning, and the next instant Joe disappeared over the side.

"Man overboard!" sang out the tug captain, as he rushed from the pilot house, for the craft was not moving. "Lower a boat!"

There came a confused jangle of bells from the other craft, but ere they had ceased vibrating, Blake Stewart had rushed forward, deserting his machine, and plunged into the waters of the bay after his chum.

"Plucky chap!" cried the captain, and even the rival skipper could not withhold a word of praise.

"We don't need a boat!" called one of the sailors on the tug Joe and Blake had hired. "They're afloat now, and I'll throw 'em a rope. He's got him!"

"Good!" cried the captain, as he rushed forward with a coil of rope. A glance over the side showed that Blake had caught Joe under one arm and was supporting him. But there was hardly any necessity for this, as Joe was a good swimmer, only the shock and suddenness of his plunge had stunned him for a moment.

"Catch hold!" ordered the captain, and a moment later Joe had his hands on the rope, being quickly hauled aboard, for he had fallen close to his own tug. Then Blake, who had managed to cling to part of the woven rope buffer, was pulled up.

"I'll have you ruled out of this harbor for that!" shouted our heroes' captain, shaking his fist at the other. "I've had enough of your mean tricks, Tom Carr!"

"Aw, I didn't mean to!" growled the other. "I gave the wrong signal, that's all. I meant to go astern and pulled the go ahead bell."

"That's all right. I've heard of your mistakes before, and this is one too often. Are you boys hurt?"

"Not a bit," answered Joe. "Only wet."

"Then get below and strip. I can lend you some clothes until the engineer dries yours."

"Not much!" cried Blake. "We can dry off later. We must finish taking these pictures. We won't get cold."

"Plucky boys!" murmured the captain, as the two lads hurried back to their machines, and, dripping wet as they were, continued to work the handles. The burning ship was now a grand if fearsome sight. She was ablaze from stem to stern; and her iron sides were getting red-hot. The small boats had taken off all the men, and were now being pulled toward some of the other craft in the harbor.

Joe made pictures of these scenes, while Blake gave his attention to the blazing ship. They had time but for a glance at the craft of their rivals, and saw that the other moving picture men were also busy reeling off films.

Then the *New Yorker,* which had gone out of sight behind the burning craft, again steamed into view, and Blake snapped her, with water spouting from her pumps. Suddenly the streams stopped, and the big fire-fighting boat headed directly for the tug on which were our heroes.

"I wonder what's up now?" thought Blake. There came a hail:

"Get back! Get back! She's going to blow up! Chemicals and alcohol in the hold! Get back! We can't save her!"

"An explosion!" yelled Blake. "We must get that, Joe."

"And I must get out of the way!" said the captain.

"Don't go any farther back than you have to," begged Joe. "We want to stay as close as we can to get good views."

"Those boys beat all I ever saw!" commented the seaman, as he rang the bell to go astern.

The *New Yorker* was steaming away to warn the other tug. The one on which the boys were had not gotten very far back from the burning ship, when she was rocked by a tremendous concussion. A volcano of fire and smoke shot up amidships from the doomed craft. Her sides seemed to bulge outward, and a great wave rose up. Then she disappeared from sight.

"I got it!" yelled Joe, steadying himself and his machine against the rocking of the tug.

"So have I!" cried Blake. "And just in time, too, for I'm at the end of my reel."

"I'm going to run for it!" yelled the captain. "There'll be a hail of fire in a few seconds!"

"Let her go!" ordered Joe. "We're done!"

The tug steamed at full speed ahead out of the danger zone, and even then some pieces of debris fell on her deck, as well as a number of burning embers that had been tossed high by the explosion, but they were quickly extinguished by the crew.

"New York as fast as we can get there!" suggested Blake, a little later. "We want to get these pictures ready for the shows."

"Say, you're as quick as the newspaper reporters," remarked the captain. "Have you got time to dry off now?"

The boys had, after packing their machines, and by the time they reached the Battery their clothes were fairly comfortable. They lost no time in hastening to the office, where they found Mr. Hadley wondering what had become of them, for they had forgotten to leave a note saying where they were going.

However, when he heard about the burning ship, he guessed that they were covering that assignment. He complimented them highly on their work, and wanted to take some action against the other tug, but the boys said it would be hard to prove that it was not an accident, though they believed the ramming had been done purposely to spoil some of the pictures.

As it was, one reel of the explosion was spoiled, for some reason or other; but Joe's was a fine one, and that night many theatre patrons had the pleasure of seeing the sensational end of the blazing steamer.

"Something new for to-day," remarked Mr. Hadley to the boys a few days later, during which time they had been making what they called "ordinary" views, being devoid of excitement.

"What is it?" asked Blake. "Anything like that trolley wreck?" for the day before he had snapped a trolley car that had been rammed by an auto, no one being hurt, as fortunately happened.

"No; something harder to get than that. It's a balloon ascension."

"A balloon!" cried Joe. "How are we going to get that if it's up in the air? I don't know as I——"

"Oh, you won't have to get in an aeroplane, though I may ask you to some day," broke in the photographer. "This time you'll snap the balloon from the ground. You'll take two machines —one a long distance camera, and, after you have gotten the ascension, with the ordinary machine, use the long distance one to snap the balloonist in the air."

"Oh, that's all right!" said Blake, wondering if the time would ever come when they would make pictures from an aeroplane.

"When is it?" asked Joe.

"To-morrow morning. I'll give you all the particulars."

Behold then, next morning, Joe and his chum setting off for a large open space of land, across the Hudson, and west of the Jersey shore, where the balloon ascension was to take place.

CHAPTER XXII

AN EXPLOSION IN MID-AIR

"SAY, there's a good crowd here!" exclaimed Joe, as they alighted from the auto they had hired, at the place of the balloon ascension.

"I should say so," agreed his chum. "We'll have some trouble getting a good view, I'm afraid."

"Oh, Mr. Hadley said to see Mr. Hotchkiss, who was manager for the balloonist, and he'd fix us up."

"Then we'd better look for him."

"That's right. I wonder if our rivals will be on hand?"

"I shouldn't be surprised," responded Blake. "This stunt has been pretty well advertised, and they must have heard of it. Trust them not to lose any tricks."

"That's so. They're pushing us hard lately, what with trying to spoil our films at the steamer fire, and wanting to keep us away from the bridge jumper."

"Oh, but we put it all over them in the trick pictures," spoke Blake. "They haven't been able to get anything like those we had. I understand they even tried to hire C. C. away from the company."

"You don't mean it! They must be hard pressed. But C. C. Piper won't go, will he?"

"Not much. But I guess we'd better stop talking and get to work. That's the balloon over there. It's one of the hot-air variety, I guess."

The boys walked through the crowd to where a big, half rounded shape could be seen bulging above the earth, swaying to and fro in the wind. They left their moving picture machines in the auto until they decided on a place from which to make the snap shots.

In a little while they had located Mr. Hotchkiss, the manager of the balloonist, who greeted the boys pleasantly.

"I have had an elevated stand built for the moving picture firms," he said. "It is over there," and he indicated it, "placed where you can have the sun at your backs, and get a good view. And I must ask you to remain until the very end of the exhibition. Don't leave after you see the balloonist up in the air."

"Why not?" asked Joe.

"Because Professor Blackwell is going to demonstrate some of his latest theories in regard to air currents, and the like. You will see a novel sight if you remain."

"Oh, we'll be here," declared Blake.

"And I think we'd better be getting over to that stand," put in Joe.

"Why?" asked his chum. "The balloon isn't half filled yet. There's lots of time."

"No, there isn't," insisted Joe. "That stand is only about big enough for our two machines, and if our rivals get there first we'll be out of it."

"That's right. Go ahead. I'm with you."

They hurried to the waiting auto, and soon were planting the two moving picture cameras on the temporary stand, which was well up over the heads of the crowd. They were only just in time, too, for a little later the manager of the rival concern came bustling up.

"Here, you boys will have to get out of that!" he snapped.

"Oh, we will?" asked Blake, calmly.

"Yes. I want that for my machine."

"Well, you won't get it!" came from Joe. "This is a free stand, and we got here first."

"I'll appeal to the manager!"

"Go ahead. We're going to stick!"

The man hastened off to find Mr. Hotchkiss,

but the latter was so busy arranging the final details of the ascent that all he said was:

"I can't settle those disputes. I built the stand for any moving picture concern that wanted to use it. First come, first served, is my motto."

"I'll make them get down!" snapped the angry rival of our heroes.

He went back to the stand and threatened to throw Joe and Blake bodily off the platform, and their machines after them. But the boys did not quail, and the presence of a police officer, who winked significantly at the lads, showed them that they would be protected.

Mr. James Munson, the rival moving picture man, pleaded and stormed, but to no avail. The boys would not give way. They did push their machines as far to one side as was practicable, and made room for another camera, but Mr. Munson refused to take advantage of this half-loaf, and hired a big truck from which to get some views. But it was not a satisfactory stand, and Joe and Blake were glad they had arrived early.

Meanwhile, the balloon was being filled with hot air. A fire had been built on the ground, some distance away from the cloth bag, and the hot air and smoke from it were led to the balloon by means of covered trenches and a pipe. This was to prevent any sparks from entering the air-craft.

Professor Blackwell had dressed in his spangled suit, and was looking after his parachute, for he was going to cut loose from his balloon when high in the air and make a descent. He also fastened a small package to the trapeze bar of his balloon.

"I guess we'd better begin making views now," suggested Joe, after a bit. "She's nearly full."

"Go ahead," said Blake. "I'll be ready to use the long-distance machine when he gets up."

The preparations went forward rapidly now. The balloon was soon filled with the hot air, and the crowd had hard work holding it until they got the word to let go.

Professor Blackwell took his position, and Joe focussed his machine on the balloonist. One last look, to see that all was in readiness, and the navigator of the air called:

"Watch what happens when I get up!"

"He's afraid we'll miss something," murmured Blake. "I wonder what's on?"

"We'll soon know," spoke his chum.

"Let go!" suddenly cried the balloonist, and the men and boys who had been holding down the tugging air-craft leaped back. Up shot the balloon, with the professor waving his hand to the crowd from the cross-bar.

Joe industriously turned the crank, getting picture after picture of the up-shooting balloon, the crowd and all the scenes leading to the ascension.

"You'd better start in now, Blake," said Joe, after a bit. "He's about out of my range now."

"Here she goes!" exclaimed Blake, and he trained his long-distance machine on the floating balloon. As it went higher and higher, of course it appeared smaller and smaller, until it was but a speck in the sky. But the perfected machine, which Mr. Hadley had supplied, could greatly enlarge the image, making it appear of good size.

The crowd was gazing upward. The balloon seemed but a little black speck in the sky. The boys were wondering what was going to happen.

Suddenly there was a distinct concussion. A black cloud enveloped the balloon, and from it shot streaks of flame.

"An explosion!" yelled a score of voices.

"He's blown up!"

"An explosion in mid-air!"

"He'll be killed!"

"Oh, I hope he doesn't fall near here!"

"So that's what he wanted us to wait for!" cried Joe. "I wonder if that was an accident, or if he did it on purpose?"

"I don't know," answered his chum; "but whatever it was, I got it, and I'm going to get him when he comes down," and he kept on turning the handle of his machine.

CHAPTER XXIII

THE FACE AT THE WINDOW

FEARING some debris from the explosion might fall on them, or that the balloonist's body might land in their midst, the crowd began to scatter.

"This is just what we want—I mean having the crowd thin out!" exclaimed Joe. "What do you think happened, Blake?"

"I don't know. There was an explosion—that's sure. The balloon is blown to pieces."

"But what of the professor? Can you see him?"

"Something's shooting down. Whether it's just the parachute alone, or——"

"It's him!" cried Joe. "The parachute has opened!"

This was true. As the boys watched, they saw the big, umbrella-shaped contrivance spread itself to catch the air, and, clinging to it, was the figure of a man.

"I guess it was just a trick," spoke Blake, as he continued to turn the handle of his machine. "I don't know what he expected to prove by the explosion, but he evidently meant it to go off just when it did. Perhaps it cut loose the parachute for him."

"Maybe," assented Joe.

"Anyhow, I've got a lot of dandy views!" declared Blake. "If he'll only land near here now, it will complete a wonderful series for the moving picture newspaper. I hope the crowd will keep back."

The throng of persons showed no inclination to get in a spot in which the balloonist might land. They were satisfied now that it was not an accident to the balloon, but a preconceived trick, and there were murmurs of wonder at the daring of the aeronaut.

"What are the other fellows doing?" asked Blake, not wanting to turn around to look at his rivals. He needed to keep his camera focused on the descending parachute with its human load, for the range was constantly changing and he had to be continually lowering the lens of his apparatus.

"They don't seem to be doing anything," replied Joe. "They are having a dispute, as near as I can make out. Something seems to have gone wrong with their machine."

"Probably they can't take in such a long range, up in the air," suggested the other lad. "It's a good thing Mr. Hadley had us take the second camera."

"That's right. Say, he's going to land in a few seconds, Blake."

"I believe you. Well, I'm ready for him. It's good there's no wind, for he won't drift off anywhere. He'll come down nearly in the place he went up from!"

Nearer and nearer the earth came the aeronaut. By this time the rival moving picture men, finding the subject now within the range of their camera, were industriously grinding away.

"Here he comes!" cried the crowd, and some of them pressed farther back to get out of the way.

There was a whistling in the air as it rushed out of the small opening in the top of the parachute.

"One side! One side!" yelled the balloonist's manager. "Don't get in his way!"

And then, when it seemed that the man would make a fair landing on an open space, there came a puff of wind that tossed him toward a clump of trees.

"He's going into them!" cried Joe.

"It looks so!" agreed his chum. "Well, it will make a better picture, though it won't be so nice for him."

The boys were not heartless, but they were getting in the same habit as does a newspaper reporter.   They looked on all happenings as for the especial benefit of their journal, no matter what the occurrence.

"He'll be killed!"

"It's all up with him now!"

"I don't see why men risk their lives in such things!"

These were some of the comments of the crowd as the balloonist shot toward the trees.

The next instant he had crashed into the branches, and with a ripping, tearing sound his parachute collapsed.

"Got him?" yelled Joe.

"I sure have!" cried Blake.   "I hope he isn't hurt much."

With the usual desire to get as near as possible to the scene of an accident, the crowd rushed forward.   In vain the balloonist's manager and his assistants tried to keep them back.   But all this made good material for the moving picture boys, and as Joe's machine was better adapted to take views now, he started his apparatus.

"It's all up with him!" shouted several.

"He's a goner!" agreed others.

"Serves him right," spoke a cross-grained man who had been near the scene of the accident.   "If folks takes their lives in their hands they deserve to get punished.   I never see such goings-on as there is nowadays. Autos and airships and balloons! It's scandalous," but with all that the man was as eager as any one else to get as near as possible, and see what had happened.

The balloonist, once he found he was headed for the trees, had braced himself to meet the shock, and, with the collapse of his frail apparatus, he had let go of it and grabbed a tree branch.

His hold was broken, and, as he crashed on downward, through the foliage, he pluckily continued to make a grab for whatever he could reach, trying, thus, to break the force of his fall.

"Say, this is right in our line!" cried Joe, "but it's so exciting that I don't know whether I'm turning the crank or not!"

"Don't you dare to forget to turn it!" exclaimed his chum. "We want every picture of this we can get," and he looked anxiously at Joe, who continued to grind away.

"Get under there, somebody, and catch him!" cried the manager of the balloonist, rushing up. "Haven't you got a net somewhere?"

"Every balloonist ought to carry his own net," remarked Blake, as he watched the struggle of the man in the tree to hold on and not slip to the ground. He was making a plucky effort, and the crowd looked on anxiously, while his manager rushed about frantically.

"There! He's got a hold!" cried the man who had made the remarks about reckless persons. "Don't fall now!" and he stationed himself under the place where the aeronaut could be observed through the leafy branches of the tree. "Hold on, for mercy's sake!"

"I guess he'll hold on for his own," observed Blake, grimly.

"Oh, just my luck!" suddenly cried Joe, as he ceased working the handle of the machine.

"What is it?" asked Blake, anxiously.

"Film's busted. Say, ask him to stay in the tree until I can fix it, and we'll have a complete picture!"

"It's a nervy thing to do, but I'll take a chance," said Blake, as he rushed over to the crowd, while his chum worked frantically to mend the broken strip of celluloid.

"Are you all right?" called Blake, to the balloonist, as he saw him astride of a limb.

"Yes; I've finally stopped falling."

"Can you stay there a little while?"

"I guess so. But what for? Don't you think I've had about enough?"

The persons in the crowd looked at Blake curiously, as he went on to explain:

"The film in our moving picture machine has broken, and it will take a minute or two to fix it.

If you can hold yourself there we can go on in a little while."

"All right, young man," was the answer. "I'll hold on. Tell me when to come down."

"I will," said Blake, as he hurried back to his chum. Joe had opened the camera, taking care not to let any light into either the exposed or unexposed film boxes. He pulled out a little of the unexposed film, fastened it to the broken end of that already exposed, losing a few pictures, of course, and then, closing the camera, again was once more ready for business.

"Go ahead!" he called.

"Give me a hand to get down," said the balloonist. "I'm all scratched up and stiff."

Some men climbed the tree and assisted the balloonist down. He did not seem to be much hurt, and in a little while he came limping toward Joe and Blake, the camera faithfully recording his approach. He was smiling and bowing in response to the applause that greeted the completion of his plucky if foolhardy feat.

"What did I tell you?" he asked of the lads. "Did I not give you a sensation?"

"You certainly did!" exclaimed Blake, who was packing up his machine, since it would be no longer needed.

"That was dynamite I exploded," explained the

balloonist. "I wanted to see if there was any danger to an aeronaut in case he was carrying bombs during war time and one of them went off before it should. I have proved that with a parachute an airman can escape."

"Well, you did, at any rate," said Blake, grimly.

"Yes. A sprained ankle is nothing. When will your pictures be ready?"

"To-night."

"So soon? I must go to New York and see them," and with a farewell wave of his hand the balloonist walked off.

"Well, I guess we might as well be going," remarked Joe, as he finished taking views and closed up his camera. "It is a little late, but I think we can get these out in time."

They were soon at their auto, which had waited for them near a roadhouse on the turnpike that led to the New York ferry. As the boys were storing their machines away, Blake happened to look toward the hostelry. He saw a face at the window—a face among many, for the place was filled with those who had come out to see the balloon ascension. At the sight of this face Blake cried out:

"Joe, there he is!"

"Who?"

"The autoist who ran down Mrs. Randolph! We must get him! Come on!" and he dashed for the hotel, followed by his chum.

CHAPTER XXIV

THE PURSUIT

"Did he see you?" asked Joe.

"I don't know whether he did or not. We've got a good chance to get him. Come on!"

"There's his auto!" cried Joe, pointing to the low-hung drab car parked with the others at the side of the hotel. "If he ever gets into that, we'll never see more than his dust."

"I don't know about that!" replied Blake, as he made a dash for the entrance. "The auto we came out in was once a racing machine. It's been made over into a touring car, but it's got the same engine. If we have half a chance, that reward is ours, Joe."

"Go on! I'm with you!" cried his chum.

The chauffeur whom they had engaged looked after the lads in some astonishment, as did many in the throng, who wondered what the moving picture boys were doing now. But Joe and Blake did not stop to tell.

Before they had entered the hotel Blake noted that the face had disappeared from the window.

194

He had a glimpse of the man looking in affright at the lads he must have known were after him.

Into the main room, where many men were gathered, dashed Blake and his chum. They looked eagerly around. There was no trace of the man they sought.

"Where is he?" cried Blake.

"Who?" asked one of the waiters.

"That man—the one who was at the window."

"There were a lot of them there," said the serving man. "I don't know which one you mean."

"The one who came in that car—the big gray racing car, out there."

"Oh, him—he just went out," spoke the waiter. "Doubtless he will be back. Do you wish to order dinner?"

"Dinner? Dinner nothing!" cried Joe. "We're not going to eat until we get that man! Come on, Blake!"

The boys rushed from a side entrance only in time to see the man crank up his auto, leap in and drive slowly from the hotel yard.

"Hold on, there!" cried Blake.

"Stop him!" shouted Joe.

The fleeing autoist paid no attention to them, but settled himself in the seat of his low, rakish racing car, and grasped the steering wheel with firm grip. Those to whom the lads appealed looked curiously at the sight of two boys running after the auto, but made no effort to stop the man who was getting away.

"Come on!" gasped Blake. "Our only chance is in the car we came in."

"But what about the pictures? We ought to send them to Mr. Hadley to be developed and printed. He's counting on them for to-night."

"That's so! What can we do? We must get that man. It may be our last chance. I have it!"

"What?"

"We'll hire some one to take the machines and reels to New York, and we'll have one of the men here telephone to Mr. Hadley, telling him about what happened. He'll understand."

"Good! I guess that will answer. But, oh, Blake, hurry! He's getting away!"

"Yes, but he isn't going as fast as he usually does. Maybe he doesn't think we have a car that can get near his, or maybe his motor doesn't work just right. Come on, it won't take but a minute!"

They quickly explained to their chauffeur what their plan was.

"I'm with you to the finish!" he cried. "There's a friend of mine here with a taxicab. He'll take your machines and pictures back to the office for you and explain things. You won't have to bother about telephoning."

"Good!" cried Blake, knowing this would save considerable time. "Get busy, then!"

It took only a few seconds to transfer the cameras and film boxes to the other machine, and the chauffeur of it readily agreed, for a fat fee, to transport them safely to the theatrical studio, and explain matters.

"Now we're off!" cried Joe, making a leap for their car, and Blake followed.

"Got plenty of gasoline?" asked the latter, of their chauffeur.

"Yes; I filled up the tank while I was waiting for you boys to get through taking pictures. I can run all night, if we have to."

"I'm hoping we won't have to," replied Blake. "But we'll keep after this fellow until we catch him. It's the best chance we've had yet, and we don't want to miss him!"

"This is a long road," said the chauffeur, "and it goes almost anywhere, with lots of side branches. It's going to be no easy job to chase this fellow."

"We'll do the best we can, and inquire at every branch road," decided Joe. "Let her go!"

The chauffeur, who had been in a number of races before he hired out as a touring car man, turned on the power, threw in the gears and released the clutch. With a jerk that told of her great reserve force, the big car shot forward. It was still early in the day, and down the road could be seen the dust of the escaping auto.

"Do you think you can get up to him?" asked Blake, as he held on to the side of the seat, for the machine was swaying in the road.

"I believe I can—if we don't get pulled in for speeding," was the answer. "This car can go some."

"That's what we want!" exclaimed Joe. "Oh, if we can get this fellow, won't Mrs. Randolph be glad!"

"And so will we," added Blake.

Faster and faster went the pursuing auto. It was clear, now, of the press of machines that had taken crowds out to see the balloon ascension, and the road was good. Faster and faster it went, following the cloud of dust in advance that hid from view the escaping autoist. Would the boys get their man and win the reward?

CHAPTER XXV

THE REWARD

"Any trace of him, Joe?"

"Yes; they say he went down this road about fifteen minutes ago."

"Fifteen minutes! Then we're gaining on him. Keep going, old man," and Blake looked pleased.

They had been on the chase for two or three hours now, and had lost considerable time stopping at crossroads and forks to inquire which way the big racing machine had gone. At times they had been able to trace its course by the marks of the peculiar, non-skidding tires in the dust of the highway. They had just stopped at a farmhouse to make further inquiries, and had learned what Joe had reported.

On they went again, the racing car that had been converted into a touring machine making good time. As Blake had said, they had made a slight gain.

"We have a good chance to catch him now," said the chauffeur. "This is a long, straight road,

199

with only little side paths leading off from it, and he won't dare to try to take them at the speed he's been using. I think we may catch him."

"I hope so," said Joe.

"The same here!" echoed Blake.

On they dashed. The afternoon was waning, but they had no thought of stopping for lunch. They got a drink of water once, when it was necessary to halt and fill the radiator of their car, but that was all.

At one point a man, evidently a constable. shouted something about speeding after them, but they kept on.

"We may run into a speed trap along here," said the chauffeur.

"Well, it'll be as bad for him as for us," rejoined Joe.

"Keep on," advised Blake, and they did.

They had covered many miles, and were almost beginning to despair of making the capture, when, as they swung around a turn in the road, Joe gave a cry and pointed ahead.

"There he is!" he shouted.

"I believe you!" declared Blake, trying to pierce the cloud of dust.

"That's him, all right," cried the chauffeur. "Here's where I use the last ounce of juice!"

He swung his gasoline lever over to the limit,

and adjusted his spark. The big car shot ahead on the level as it had not done before that day.

"He's trying to leave us!" yelled Joe. "He's cut out his muffler!"

"We can do the same, and gain a little," said the chauffeur. The thunder of the explosions, unhampered by the muffler, drowned talk. Ahead was the drab racing car, seeming to draw away from its pursuers.

Suddenly, there was a loud explosion. The forward car was seen to swerve sharply to one side, run up the bank, and then almost turn turtle. The man was thrown out and lay still at the side of the road.

"The chase is over!" yelled the boys' chauffeur. "He threw a shoe, and it's lucky he wasn't killed. We have him now!"

"Maybe he is killed!" exclaimed Blake, but this was disproved a moment later, for the man got slowly up and limped to a stump, where he sat down.

"Well, you've got me," he said simply, as the boys came up. "I can't run with a sprained ankle. I was foolish to keep away, anyhow, for I'm sorry about that smash-up of the old lady, and I'm willing to pay damages. I give up."

"Well, we got you at last!" exclaimed Blake, with an air of relief.

"Yes, and I've got you!" exclaimed another voice, and a man, evidently a constable, came running up the road. "I'm Constable Jim Teeter of Arlingburg Township," he went on; "and my partner, Sam Eaton, of Analomick, telephoned me that you was headed this way, burnin' up the roads. I've got you!"

"What do you want with us?" asked Blake. "We haven't done anything, except chase after this man—for whom we've been looking for a long time."

"I want you for speeding," replied the officer. "I've seen and heard of some autoists goin' pretty fast, but you folks are the limit! Why, children and chickens ain't safe in the roads with such drivin' goin' on as you folks have been guilty of! You've got to come with me!"

"Then if we're guilty he is, too!" exclaimed Joe, pointing to the man whose car had smashed. "We were chasing him."

"Yes; a regular road race, I take it," went on the constable, as he made a grab for Blake's sleeve. "We've heard them stories before. One man starts fast, and the other man doesn't like his dust, so he tries to get ahead, and they both use all the speed they've got. We've heard of such cases before. Now you've got to come along with me and pay your fines, all of you."

"I'm willing to. I admit I was speeding," said the man, as he looked at the boys and smiled slightly, as though he was not at all sorry to get them into the same trouble as that in which he found himself.

"Ha! So you plead guilty, do you?" cried the constable. "Waal, that may make it easier on you when you come afore the judge. But you fellers," and he turned to the moving picture boys, "you fellers will have to——"

"What's this coming?" cried Blake, as they heard a sound down the road, and saw a cloud of dust approaching.

"It's another pesky autoist!" cried the constable. "I'm in luck to-day. I'll pull him in and arraign you all at once. This is a regular harvest!" and, letting go of Blake's sleeve, the officer caught up a big fence rail and made his way to the middle of the road.

"What are you going to do?" cried Joe.

"Stop that auto!" was the answer.

"How?"

"Chuck this rail through the spokes of the wheel. That will bring 'em up short enough."

"Yes, and maybe make the car turn turtle, and cause a loss of life," objected Blake. "If you want to stop that car get out in the middle of the road and hold up your arms."

"And get run over?" asked the constable.

"I guess they'll stop," spoke Joe. "Go ahead. But don't try such a risky thing as thrusting a rail in the wheels. You might be hurt yourself."

"I wouldn't want that to happen," said the constable, and, throwing aside the rail, he stepped out into the highway, waving his arms like windmill sails.

"Stop!" he yelled. "Hold on there! I arrest you for speedin'!"

"As if they could hear him," remarked Joe.

"They're coming on slow, for an auto," said Blake, and, truly, the cloud of dust did not advance very rapidly.

"Maybe they have had an accident," suggested Joe, and then, as the wind shifted and the dust-cloud blew aside, they saw that it was no auto, but a rattly sort of carriage drawn by an old horse who was being urged on at top speed by a man.

"By heck!" cried Constable Jim Teeter. "It's Sam Eaton—the constable that telephoned to me about you folks. How'd you get here, Sam?" he asked.

"Hopped into Squire Black's rig, as soon as I telephoned to you," was the answer. "I made this old hoss cover the ground, too. Did you nab 'em all right?"

"I sure did."

"Waal, don't forgit that half th' reward and fine comes to me."

"I won't," answered the first man, as he walked back to where the boys and the autoist waited. "What have you got to say?" he asked, while the other constable looked on. "Why was you chasin' this man?"

Blake soon explained.

"But you was speedin', all the same," went on the second constable. "That doesn't excuse you. How do you plead?" and he assumed the air of a judge.

"We plead guilty," said Blake, simply. "We were after this man, for whom we have a warrant." And he extended the legal document he had always carried; also some of the enlarged pictures of the man.

"There's no need for this," said the injured autoist. "I admit my recklessness."

"Waal, I'll take ye all into custody, I guess," went on Jim Teeter. "Then it'll be all reg'lar, an' I'll git my fees. Better come along to th' jedge."

The matter was soon arranged. In the boys' auto, for the other was temporarily out of commission, the hurt autoist was taken before the nearest magistrate. The moving picture boys pleaded guilty to speeding and were fined ten dollars, which they paid. The same procedure was had in the case of Penfield Jetson, which the autoist gave as his name. The boys recognized it as that of a professional who had won many big races by his reckless speed.

Mr. Jetson gave a bond in the matter of the complaint of Mrs. Randolph, and announced that there would be no necessity of prosecuting him, as he would pay all damages.

"I'm sorry for what happened," he said; "and I'm glad that lady wasn't hurt. You boys kept on my track pluckily."

"I guess you'd have done the same if there was five hundred dollars in it!" exclaimed Blake.

"Five hundred dollars!" cried the constable. "Is there that much money in the world? I wish I'd a seen this feller first, boys!"

The legal matters thus being settled, the parties were all allowed to go, and, now that they found Mr. Jetson was not such a bad character, though rather reckless, the boys took him back to New York with them.

"What are you going to do with that reward when you get it?" the autoist asked of the lads.

"Buy a moving picture camera and go into business for ourselves!" exclaimed Joe.

"That's what!" echoed Blake; "and we're going to get some rare views, too!"

And how they did this will be related in the

next volume of this series, to be called, "The Moving Picture Boys in the West; Or, Taking Scenes Among the Cowboys and Indians."

"Well, we did it," said Joe that night, when he and his chum had reached the studio, and found that the pictures of the balloon ascension had safely arrived, proving most excellent.

"We sure did," agreed his chum. "And most of it through luck, too."

"Not all," said Mr. Hadley, who had heard the story. "I give you boys credit for hard work, too. I wish you were going to stay here with me, but I admit there is a bigger field out West for you."

"Oh, we're not going to sever all connection with you," declared Joe. "We'll want your firm to market our pictures for us. And we'd be glad to have you with us."

"Indeed we would!" assented Blake.

"Going out West, eh?" mused C. C. Piper, who had heard of the boys' resolve. "Well, if you're not scalped by the Indians, the cowboys will get you into a cattle stampede. You'll wish you'd never gone."

"Oh, forget it, Gloomy," advised Mr. Hadley. "Tell us it's going to rain."

"It is!" declared the moody comedian, as he washed off the clown's paint from his face. "I'm sure something is going to happen before morning. I feel it in my bones."

"Something is going to happen!" declared Blake.

"What?" they all asked, in some apprehension.

"I'm going to have my supper. I'm nearly starved. Come on, Joe, and we can talk about spending that reward when Mrs. Randolph sends it to us."

And thus, with pleasant anticipations before them, we will, for the time being, take leave of the moving picture boys.

THE END